RETRO HORROR
an anthology

Nightmare Press
Louisville, KY

Copyright © 2020 by Nightmare Press
All Rights Reserved

Edited by Jacob Floyd
Cover Art and Graphic Design by Luke Spooner

No portion of this book may be copied or transmitted in any form, electronic or otherwise, without express written consent of the publisher or authors.

This book is a work of fiction. Names, characters, locations, events, and incidents are fictitious and are used fictitiously. Any resemblance to any actual people (living or dead), places, events, or incidents is unintentional and purely coincidental.

Thank you for reading! If you like the book, please leave a review on Amazon and Goodreads. Reviews help authors and publishers spread the word.

To keep up with more Nightmare Press news, join the Anubis Press Dynasty on Facebook.

The Frightening Floyds, Jenny and Jacob Floyd, would like to dedicate this collection to Jacob's sister, Carly, and brother-in-law, Glenn, for all the exposure to low-budget and old-school horror films. Those days are what started the love for the genre.

YEARS OF HOPE AND DARKNESS
foreword by Jim Towns

The eighties were an amazing decade to be alive in. And they were a terrifying decade to live through, as well.

I started the eighties as a Kindergartener and finished them as an adolescent, and I can attest that there's a reason the word *awesome* became such a common catchphrase during this time - because it was the only word to adequately describe so many seemingly bigger-than-life events that took place over those ten years. *Awesome* is, after all, a neutral phrase: it can describe both splendor and horror; it applies just as well to a carpet-bombing as it does to the execution of a perfect 360. And that's the kind of watchword these years required. The decade had dawned with Americans held hostage in a foreign land, but a handsome and energetic new president had (to all outward appearances) swept into office and made sure they were brought home safe. John Lennon, co-founder of the most successful musical group of the century, was slain in the first year of the eighties, but Paul McCartney was soldiering on – and was even doing duets with Michael Jackson. Neil Diamond was singing about *E.T.*, and Prince was the star of his very own film, so it couldn't be that bleak, right?

That's what people told themselves. But just like any fable worth its salt, there was a darkness lurking just beneath the surface of it all.

The Race to Space had all-but ended, and the Cold War was heating up like it hadn't in years. The ever-present threat of mutually assured annihilation by nuclear weapons was inescapable; it infiltrated into news, literature, and of course, film. Even as a new surge of patriotism swept through the U.S., we lived under the constant fear that our species was always one button away from extinction.

So we diverted ourselves. The eighties beheld one of the most incredible outputs of beloved art and entertainment of any decade in the Twentieth Century. And it's little surprise that output mirrored the duality of hope and terror that permeated daily life: for every *E.T.*, there was a *John Carpenter's The Thing*. One could groove to Phil Collins or Sheena E, or else tread on the dark side with Mötley Crüe, Slayer or Public Enemy. Kids my age grew up obsessed with *Star Wars* and *The Muppets*, while simultaneously being fascinated with ninjas. In fact almost every one of my friends (including me) had a small arsenal of throwing stars secreted away where their parents couldn't find them – just in case things got bad – because it was the eighties and even as kids we knew that was always a possibility.

Let's not forget that Stephen King positively OWNED the eighties. His (occasionally cocaine-fueled) output during these years was nothing short of inhuman. It honestly seemed like there was a new King novel out on the bookstands every seventeen days. Critical works like *Firestarter*, *Cujo*, *Pet Sematary*, *It* and *Misery* established his dominance as the voice of literary horror for the decade – a decade that saw the rise of many other great horror writers like Clive Barker, Dean Koontz and more.

In cinema, horror inarguably had its greatest decade since the heydays of the 1930s classic monster flicks. To list all the iconic horror films and franchises that the decade birthed into the world would stretch this introduction beyond the point of reason: suffice to say the decade saw a new genesis of monsters and villains so indelible that many of these films have, for forty years now, been in a near-perennial state of remakes.

But to my mind, there are two works of horror which best epitomize this fractured decade: one is a feature film series, the other a piece of fiction that would later become both a film and a series as well. Neither is my absolute favorite example of its creator's oeuvre, but both capture the feel of the era as well as any.

Wes Craven's *A Nightmare on Elm Street* franchise capitalized on previous works like Peter Benchley's *Jaws* and the Tobe Hooper/Steven Spielberg film *Poltergeist*, in bringing horror right home to the focal point of 1980s culture: the suburbs. Murderer Freddy Krueger escapes the law but meets his fate at the hands of PTA mob violence, and is burned alive. He returns years later, however, to haunt the mob's (now teenage) children's dreams: killing them off one by one as they slumber. His attacks come in the surreal and abstract mindscape of the dream world – his manifestations are infinite. For his sleep-deprived prey, the barriers between reality and fantasy soon become impossible to distinguish. Nowhere is safe. In a decade that told us you can have anything you dream, these films warned us that while that might be true, it was your dreams themselves that would kill you in the end.

The other titular work is admittedly a bit of a cheat, as the novel version of *The Dead Zone* by Stephen King was published in August of 1979: a few months before the eighties began. But I (and I'm sure many people) read it in the latter decade, and the original film version (directed by David Cronenberg) was released in 1983.

In both novel and film, everyman Johnny Smith is injured in a car accident, waking up years later to an agonizing rehabilitation, as well as a new ability to see the future. He attempts to use this power for good, but soon finds himself dreaming of a president who, in a fit of paranoia and madness, intentionally ignites a nuclear holocaust. Confronted with that very man in the form of handsome and dynamic presidential candidate Greg Stillson, Smith decides he must assassinate the man before this terrible fate comes to pass, even at the cost of his own life. While King's narrative continues to prove eerily prescient in its concept, its focus on atomic war as the ultimate boogeyman establishes its place as a touchstone piece of eighties horror. Written during one administration, the story would find its popularity during another, and anyone reading or watching couldn't help make the logical jump between the Stillson character and our own affable Commander-in-Chief, wondering what darkness might lurk behind his winning smile. Of course we would eventually find out that this man had been quietly allowing Americans to die from a deadly new virus, simply because he didn't approve of their lifestyle. Meanwhile he was happily selling weapons to murderers abroad, sitting in the Oval Office even as his own mind began to slowly betray him.

It would have been fitting if the eighties had gone out with a rousing montage rising in a crescendo to the screeching guitar of Eddie Van Halen, or perhaps to the cacophonous sounds of roaring kerosene explosions as the decade jumped a cavernous gulch in its nitro-powered muscle car, last of the V-8s, but the reality is the decade just kind of petered out into the nineties. The Berlin Wall fell and Communist Russia crumbled, so we all felt safer – for a time. A growing awareness of our role as the only remaining Superpower both humbled us and made us more arrogant. The admiration of Gordon Gecko-inspired vulture capitalism was (for some at least) replaced by a growing sense of responsibility for the care of our own fragile planet. Tastes in music and film and literature evolved, though the old mainstays of the 80s continued to enjoy regular resurgences of popularity, and in truth many of the books and movies and bands I grew up with are still my favorites today. Time is a funny thing and can, over the years, relegate even the most shocking or frightening experience to the innocuous realm of comfort food.

We look back now and smile at the seeming quaintness of period landmarks like *New Coke* and stonewashed jeans; Cyndi Lauper and *Pac Man*, *Rambo* and *My Little Pony* – and yet all these things are still with us, or like a horror movie villain, have since been resurrected into the 21st century (except for the stonewashed jeans, thankfully).

The eighties cast a very long shadow both in my own life, and in American culture as well. Some events from that era forever changed our world for the better, while others haunt us to this day. Hope and darkness are two polar opposites forever intertwined, like the double helix of our own genes: forever changing, improving, then devolving again, then rising up once more. If Mary Ann Evans was right, and history does in fact repeat itself, then I suppose there's hope.

After all, we made it through this goddamn decade once. We can do it again.

RETRO HORROR
an anthology

TABLE OF CONTENTS

1. One Monster King to Rule Them All
by Gregg Chamberlain
p. 01

2. Mothsquito
by Pedro Iniguez
p. 14

3. Dippel's Monkey
by Gordon Grice
p. 39

4. Sloth Zombies
by The Frightening Floyds
p. 55

5. Puddle of Mud: A Tale of the Bajazid
by Kenneth Bykerk
p. 80

6. Pirantulas!
by Angela Yuriko Smith
p. 96

7. The Mouth of the Deep
by Stanley B. Webb
p. 107

8. Hunting the Goat Man
by Pamela K. Kinney
p. 123

9. Crypto Cage Match
by William D. Carl
p. 131

10. The Trials of Dr. Rains
by Matthew M. Montelione
p. 150

11. Unhallowed Evening
by R.C. Mulhare
p. 169

12. The Maze
by K.J. Watson
p. 190

ONE MONSTER KING TO RULE THEM ALL
by Gregg Chamberlain

"Who is the true king of all monsters?"

The moderator leaned back from the microphone, allowing the pause to linger at the end of the question. He surveyed the sea of faces filling the Hollywood Bowl's outdoor amphitheatre. On and on the tiered rows of creatures, great and small—some human, most not—stretched from the premium-price front rows all the way through to the "cheap seats" that encircled the rim. Above them the "nosebleed" ranks of expanding bleachers towered, holding even more spectators. Above those loomed the three large long-distance camera mounts, already occupied by alert news crews from all the Big Three networks. The feeder line connection to the FOX mobile van had been exiled to the back parking lot.

That should teach Murdoch's lot a lesson about "playing nice" thought the moderator, with a snarling grin.

Another three separate camera mounts were occupied by crews from the main networks representing the rest of the world: CBC, BBC, CINÉ, Ital, Tag, ATV, the People's Network,

Japan TV, along with feeder teams from broadcast news groups like CNN, Reuters, AP, UPI, and others.

Behind the main stage and off to either side stood gigantic plasma Maxitron display screens to allow the audience members in the far back a more reasonable view of everything on the stage, such as the moderator, whose uncouth and hirsute image now filled all the screens.

A giant paw combed through the shaggy ruff of the moderator's neck fur on-screen. Far below, on stage, he leaned forward to address the microphone again.

"You've wondered, I've wondered, we've *all* wondered! Who among us all is the most monstrous, the most magnificent, the most marketed and marketable to the masses in the media-savvy world?"

The moderator paused again, then murmured in an almost casual growling tone, "Today, my friends and fiends, today, we will have our answer!"

The moderator thrust out a taloned finger, stabbing at the audience. "And you are here to witness!"

The crowd exploded in applause: roars, whistles, screams, hisses, cheers, and shrieks melded and rose, then hit a crescendo that echoed across the amphitheatre. The moderator waited for the soaring, roaring applause to dwindle, and at last die down. Strange eyes of hot amber-yellow gazed out at the audience. Black lips parted in a lupine smile, fangs flashing for a moment in the spotlight.

ONE MONSTER KING TO RULE THEM ALL

"Yes, *you* are *here*. But not just as witnesses. No! *You* here, and you out *there*—our T.V. and online audiences—you too will have your say, your voice, in deciding who is the greatest of us all—who is the King of *All* Monsters!"

A roaring ocean of applause almost drowned out the moderator's words. All manner of cheers surged and eddied around the stage. When at last it settled down to a low, continuous, moaning murmur, the moderator stepped back from the edge of the stage, microphone in one clawed hand, the other waving to the side, directing the audience's attention to a trio seated stage-right at the far end of the amphitheatre shell.

"And now, our panel of judges, creatures of the night and from beyond the pale. They need no introduction but, to satisfy protocol and for the benefit of our viewers out there less-than-well-read on their fantastic history, we present, with great, great pride, pleasure, and panache: the Frankenstein Monster, Mr. Griffin, also known as the Invisible Man, and Milord Imhotep, better known as the Mummy!"

Frankenstein's Monster sat, erect and stiff-backed, in his chair at the table, all bulging muscles sheathed in grey, cadaverous skin. Dull matte-black hair covered the flat top of his misshapen head. Old scars dimpled his face. Crude surgical stitching crisscrossed his forehead, neck, and each exposed wrist sticking out of the threadbare sleeves of a plain coat two sizes too small for his mighty frame. He grinned at the scattered cheering from the audience that followed the announcement of his nom de guerre. Great, square, chalk-white teeth gleamed in the spotlight.

A placard flashed above the heads of the beings in the front-row seats. "We Love You, Frankie!" In response, a big, square-fingered hand lifted. Yellow-green fingers tipped with cracked and blackened nails wiggled in a shy wave, earning more applause in return.

Sitting dwarfed beside the famous product of a mad scientist's vision, Griffin's bandage-wrapped head did a slow shake of disbelief. Or it may have been disgust. Hard to say either way. Dark glasses perched atop a cloth-bound protuberance where a nose might be turned from one side to the other as the madman gazed at his tablemates, then out towards the audience. He noted no banners of welcome or placards of praise for him. Kid-gloved hands sat folded at rest on the tabletop, fingers twitching slightly. "Homicidal mania counts for bloody nothing these days," whispered unseen lips.

Imhotep sat silent and still. Once he was High Priest of Amon-Ra until an attempt at a forbidden passion for Pharaoh's daughter pulled him down from his lofty position. His enemies then made him a living mummy through the arcane arts of ancient Egyptian wizardry and condemned him to the dark depths of the tomb.

Imhotep listened and learned. Resurrected centuries later through the foolishness of arrogant men, he had stalked and slew until his own treacherous heart betrayed him once more through a mistaken infatuation with what had seemed the very reincarnation of his long-lost love and doomed him once more to a crypt-bound rest.

Imhotep watched and waited.

The moderator turned back to face the audience.

"Before introducing our two participants in this great debate, we will have a brief—and I do mean, brief—summary of the rules of procedure.

"Each of our candidates will be presented separately. They are each allowed a maximum of two minutes to introduce themselves and make an opening statement. Following that the official debate begins, with a total of half an hour for candidate exchange of arguments, comments, and criticisms. Following will be a brief recess then the open-mike question period. One minute is allowed for each question. No exceptions. Any attempt to exceed the one-minute time limit will result in a stunning blow to the head, or other appendages and attachments, from one of our monitors."

The moderator gestured down towards stage-front where a small group of hulking hooded brutes, massively-muscled arms folded across their barrel chests, stood glowering at the front rows through the eye slits of their black executioner-hood masks.

"No exceptions," repeated the moderator, lips peeling back in a lupine smile. "This is your first, last, and only warning."

He allowed a moment's silent pause to let the cautionary advice sink in.

"Question period will continue for one hour or until all questions are asked and answered, whichever happens first. Candidates have two minutes to respond to a question. Please, do *not* repeat a question already asked, or you will answer to the monitors."

The moderator paused once more. "After question period, candidates will each have two minutes for individual summaries, after which the judges will go into seclusion to consider both their own observations and the tally of audience votes."

A wolfish grin revealed sharp white teeth. "And that's where you come in! Yes, you sitting here with us today, and you out there at home in front of your living room television set, or joining us on the World Wide Web, you get to help choose the winner. While the judges are sequestered off-stage in discussion, you will have five minutes to cast your own vote. For those seated here at the Bowl, there are two buttons, one on each arm of your chair, the one on the right is red for our first speaker, the left green for our second. For our online and home audience you just have to text #VLAD or #ROAR to make your choices."

The moderator waited for the cheers and applause to die down again and the waving placards and rippling banners to sink back out of sight. The monitors spread out. One took up a position at one microphone stand set up to one side of the stage. A second took his place at another mike stand erected at the opposite end of the stage. The rest spread out into the audience to both ensure good order and assist with immediate recognition of hopeful questioners. Wherever they passed and came to a halt, the cheering was less raucous, more subdued, but still enthusiastic all the same.

"And now, we present our first candidate: once a mortal prince, now the Lord of the Undead...DRACULA!"

A long moment of dead silence, then— explosion!

Cheers, whistles, loud impassioned moans sounded; hands waved, glowsticks whipped back and forth in frenzied yellow-green streaks, thousands of flames flickered from lighters held in human and unhuman hands, and in a few cases perched on the ends of inhuman fingertips. The sea of tiny flames spread out from the edge of the stage like a fiery wave as the spotlight locked on the tall imposing figure gliding forward from beyond the far-right curtain.

One enthusiastic admirer evaded the nearest monitor and thrust up a handmade sign as the noble being passed by. Crude blood-red letters declared: I'm Down With The Count!

The regal head turned. Hooded eyes glanced down. A ghost of a smile revealed the white tip of fang. A slight nod of acknowledgement and the legend moved on, midnight-black cape billowing and curvetting like huge restless wings. No more attention given to the hapless fan as an annoyed monitor slammed a meaty fist against the back of his skull. He dropped limp to the floor and was carried off down an exit corridor for deposit into a dumpster outside.

The moderator backed away, bowing low, as the Lord of Vampires approached the microphone.

He stood a moment in silent grandeur then inclined forward, closer to the mike.

"Good evening."

The liquid tones of the rich tenor voice rippled out from the stage, over the front rows, and up the ranks of the amphitheatre audience. Women were passing out before it reached the rim of the bowl. A few men joined the fainting fit follies, along with several vampiresses, though some of those might have been vampire groupies in full formal regalia.

Dracula stepped back from the microphone, giving place to the moderator. He turned, with a swirl of his cape, and strode over to his appointed podium, complete with its own microphone setup.

The moderator allowed a full minute to pass while seatmates of the fainted helped their friends either to sit back up or head up the nearest aisle to the appropriate exit where paramedics were on standby.

"Our next candidate has been called the King almost from the day he first emerged out of the ocean depths to romp and stomp on everything and everyone almost everywhere in the world. A larger-than-life dragon legend. The inspiration for Jörmungandr, Tiamat, Python, and every great wyrm that starred in ancient song and story. Hollywood has tried to capture his image for decades since *The Beast from 20,000 Fathoms*! He is the guiding spirit behind every kaiju creation on the Big and Little Screens, videogames, and every comic book and manga that exists today. He's mean, he's green, and he's on the scene! His

ONE MONSTER KING TO RULE THEM ALL

friends and fans call him Big Guy, but the rest of the world knows him best…

An ear-shattering roar drowned out the rest of the introduction. There was also the ecstatic cheering of the audience, but that was the merest whisper, at best, in comparison to the paean of power whose reverberations rumbled around the amphitheatre. It was the sound of doom, Gabriel's Horn of Judgment made real, a call to ride fast and far in terror-stricken flight from the Apocalypse, all the while fearing that escape was futile.

Tremors rocked the ground. Spectators clung to the arm-rests of their seats. The broadcast towers rattled even as camera crews scrambled to align their lenses in the direction of the roar. The moderator on-stage and the monitors scattered around the amphitheatre all staggered but managed to remain standing. The three judges gripped the table before them.

Only Dracula appeared unaffected, unperturbed, and unimpressed by both sound and shockwave. Nothing more than a slight sneer distorted the thin line of his bloodless lips.

Directly above the amphitheatre bowl the stars in the early night-time sky winked out. A gigantic shadowy outline occluded them. The roar that sounded like a death-knell for the world slowly faded, leaving behind the faintest, though still-loud, shadow scream of excited spectators, cheering the arrival of their icon – Leviathan.

Several minutes passed before the latest thunder of applause had at last subsided, aided by the efficient and effective efforts of the monitors with the more enthusiastic audience members. The moderator glanced up towards the shadowed figure looming over the Bowl, then behind him towards the vampire nobleman standing at ease behind his own podium mike.

The moderator shook himself, snorted, growled to clear his throat before stepping back up to the main mike. Black-rimmed lips parted slightly in a fang-tipped smile.

"And now without further ado - making his introductory statement: the one, the only, the original Count Dracula!" he exclaimed, drawing out both words for the sake of showmanship.

The stage lights dimmed, except for a single spotlight centered on the podium of the vampire lord, whose head lifted slightly as he listened to the swelling roar of the audience washing over the stage to surge and crash at his immortal feet.

He smiled, held up a single hand.

Silence reigned.

"I bid you good evening, once more. I, Wladislaus Drakulya, Son of the Dragon, Son of the Devil, known to generations born after my 'death' as Vlad Tepes, Vlad the Impaler, bid you all welcome. I was born a prince of Wallachia, and ruler over Moldavia and Transylvania. I was a leader of men, a lord of armies, liege of my country by divine right. I was the scourge of the Turk, who feared me and named me Kaziklu Bey. Under my rule a lone woman could walk a dark road at midnight anywhere in my land and know she was safe from all harm. Homes and shops were unlocked at all hours for no thief or robber would dare to steal from anyone. My name alone was cause for pagan nightmares. Now my name is another word for dark… passion."

Arms swept out and up, lifting the cape like spreading wings. The still-handsome face gazed up towards the heavens.

"I am Fear. I am Death. I…am…Dracula! What giant grotesquerie from the dismal dawn of Earth can compare?"

The arms dropped, wrapping the cape in a cocoon around the vampire's tall figure. Eyes that had watched the centuries roll past now gazed out and over the crowd and into the darkness beyond. Lips lifted slightly, revealing Dracula's gleaming white canines, in a small satisfied smile as the audience went wild.

It took awhile before the applause and the cheering began to die down. The monitors did not even stir from their posts this time, as if recognizing the futility. The moderator scratched behind one ear as he waited, glancing now and again at the judges' table, at Dracula, and then above at the giant figure blocking out the stars.

"And now," said the moderator, taking charge once more, "we present our second candidate, and thanks to the latest advances in cyber-linguistics, encryption/decryption technology, we will hear him *speak*!

More cheering. More waiting. Meanwhile, standard boom mikes elevated to their apexes and "elephant ear" amplifier microphone discs swung into position. Technicians inside remote broadcast relay vans checked their monitors, confirming their links to the language decoding program as online and active.

The giant shadow shifted. TV cameras swung into new positions, tracking the enormous figure of the entity known to the ancients as Leviathan; special ultra-wide-angle zoom lenses simultaneously extended and adjusted focus. The first image they captured was a phosphorescent blue-green sheen sliding along the edges of the shadowy giant. A huge maw gaped wide. A metallic shrieking growl tore through microphone circuits and erupted from the towering speaker banks surrounding the amphitheatre.

"Hear me roar!"

Lambent blue energy arcs winked out against the sky. A blinding white column of hellfire erupted from the giant shadowy head, burned down and through the stage floor, at the same time engulfing Dracula and the podium where he stood in an eye-searing pillar of destruction.

The enormous mouth closed. The holocaust column of flame vanished, leaving behind a huge, gaping, smoking hole in the stage floor. And no vampire lord to be seen.

A moment's stunned silence, followed by immediate chaos. Panicked audience members fought to escape from the amphitheatre pit. Outraged Dracula groupies grappled with fans of his exterminator, each exchanging punches, kicks, and eye gouges. Monitors beat up everyone within range, seeking to enforce order and failing, only adding to the madness.

The moderator looked up at the still-looming bulk of the behemoth now retreating with slow earthquake-heavy steps from the Hollywood Bowl. He shook his head. "Due to circumstances beyond our control," he muttered into the mike, "the Great Debate is suspended." He regarded the riot scene in the seats. Shrugged. "Retain your ticket stubs. Refund arrangements will be made. Please exit quietly and in an orderly fashion, if you can."

At the judges' table, the Invisible Man shook his bandaged head. "Oi! Should have bloody well seen that coming."

Frankenstein's Monster nodded, his slate-grey features grimacing. "I'm working with a used and diseased brain, and even I knew this wouldn't end well."

"Rrrrmmmm mmmmm," groaned Imhotep in agreement.

MOTHSQUITO
by Pedro Iniguez

The stars were like pinholes above the black sky. Dana crossed her arms around her chest to ward off the cold desert air. She averted her gaze from Hank, afraid to make eye contact as tears streamed down her cheek.

"Please don't go, Hank," she said.

"I have to. You know that," Hank said. He was middle-aged with graying sideburns and a square jaw any superhero would have been proud to own. "I'm the only one that knows how to stop this thing."

"I-I know, but Hank, Scorpiosaurus, it's gotten too big now. I-I…"

Hank walked up to Dana and placed his finger on her mouth to shush her. He leaned in and kissed her. She gripped his back tightly, like a child refusing to relinquish her teddy bear on the first day of school.

Hank pulled away. "Now, go with Corporal Clemens and his men; they'll protect you." A young man in full tactical gear and camouflage walked up to her and placed a gentle hand on her shoulder. "As for me, I have to plant the explosives on the—"

MOTHSQUITO

The tip of a large, seven foot tail pierced Hank's abdomen and lifted him five feet off the ground. A spray of hot red liquid splattered Dana's face before she screamed. Corporal Clemens pushed her aside and along with three other soldiers swung an assault rifle to his hip and unleashed a torrent of thunderous gunfire.

Out of the shadows and into the moonlight appeared the head of a giant scorpion. Its mandibles opening and clamping violently as it neared its prey.

Hank looked up at Dana with his last breath and said, "Ouch. This thing's starting to hurt."

"Cut! goddammit, cut!" yelled a man off-screen.

Salvador "Sal" Santos lit a cigarette, leaned against a rusty trailer, and watched as Dino DeLuca, the short, stocky Italian director, waddled his way in front of the camera. Behind him, screenwriter Marty Brenner followed like a lapdog.

"What was that, Mike? What was that?" Dino said in a thick Italian accent.

Mike Miller hung suspended by thin wires as a pneumatic prosthetic tail protruded from his midsection. The fake blood had run down his plaid shirt and into the desert floor. "Sorry, Dino. The wires are really digging into my shoulders. This isn't like the soaps, you know. I've never done this kind of stuff."

Miller, a washed-up soap actor, had done nothing besides complain and make excuses for his blunders during the shoot. Sal was used to people like that, but the narcissism on set had been through the roof. He had heard most creative types had their quirks, so he had prepared himself for this.

"Mikey," Dino said, taking off his baseball cap and squeezing it in his hands. "We have a shoestring budget. We have to get this shot right. Do you know how expensive this blood is? The executives aren't going to give me more money."

"Dino?" said Carol Connors as she approached from behind.

"What is it?"

"Can we make Dana, you know, not a simpleton? I feel like maybe she's too much of a damsel in distress and not enough Ellen Ripley. Can we get her some guns?"

"No! We can't change the script, it's set in stone. The budget has already been approved. You want Ripley? Find us a better writer."

Marty Brenner glared at Dino and walked away.

"Now, Carol, go stand over there; we're doing another take. Where is that military consultant? Get his lazy ass over here!" he shouted to no one in particular as he nestled his cap back on his sweaty head.

Sal stomped out his cigarette and walked over to Dino. "Hey, what's up?"

Dino smacked his hairy arm. "Damn mosquitoes, must they torment me, too? Anyway, what did you think of that shot, Sal? Pretty brutal, eh? I thought it would look good on camera if we had continuous muzzle flashes from all four soldiers. All lights and blood; a sort of a stark contrast to the darkness of the desert."

MOTHSQUITO

"Dino, with all due respect, everything with that shot was off."

"Huh? What do you mean?"

Sal walked over to the four extras in army camo. Nate, the man who played Corporal Clemens, was slinging an Ak-47 over his shoulder.

"First off, the U.S. doesn't use these rifles, they use M16s. Second, Nate, can you and the rest of the guys remember to keep your fingers off the triggers when not in action? Third, no one fires from the hip. It's ridiculously inaccurate, dangerous, and should be left in the 80's. Fourth, you have to fire in bursts; never go full-auto. Too much recoil and before you know it, you're out of ammo. Now, I know this is a creature-feature, but come on, this is the U.S. military; our guys have a little more discipline than that."

Dino's brows furrowed and the corner of his lip curled like an angry dog. "Bah! No one here understands filmmaking." He turned from Sal and into the beam of a bright spotlight. "And someone get this freaking light out of my face before you blind the one useful person on this production!"

A stagehand turned the light off and the darkness of night enveloped the set. Only the moon and the twinkle of starlight lit the crew. It was a moment of peace and clarity for Sal. He remembered many nights like this out on training missions or when he was deployed on foreign soil. In those moments, it felt like a brief stint in Heaven before Hell broke loose.

"Okay, everyone take ten," Dino said. "Mike, get into a new set of clothes. We are getting this shot right if it kills me."

A stagehand helped Mike Miller down as Carol Connors walked into her dilapidated trailer where the barks of her vicious Chihuahua could be heard.

Sal walked over to Marty Brenner who was leaning on a van. He was sparking a marijuana pipe as the flicker of fire cast their shadows on the floor like some psychedelic ballet.

"Want a hit?" Marty asked.

"No, thanks. I find that stuff dulls the senses."

"It helps numb the pain."

Sal didn't bother asking what caused the man's pain. He just smiled and nodded.

"I've been writing since I was seventeen. It's all I ever wanted to do. The greatest joy; I mean the reason I do it, is to have someone say, 'Hey, that story was pretty good. It took me out of my problems for a little while.' Doing this shitty B-film clunker for a shitty B-film channel has been an all-time low for me. Why? Because no one takes these films seriously." He took a hit from his pipe and leaned his head back. Marty coughed and blew a cloud of smoke into the sky.

"We've all done work we're not proud of," Sal said looking around the production which consisted of a few generators, some lights, two cameras, a couple of trailers, and a few pickup trucks. "But we can't let that define us. I know you've got that one big story ahead of you." He winked and walked away from the pity party.

Near the edge of the production, Carol's trailer sat like a rusted castle; an emblem of the low-budget monstrosity of a film. Her notorious Chihuahua, Cookie, could be heard yapping away.

MOTHSQUITO

She yelled something inaudible and stepped outside.

"Everything okay, ma'am?" Sal asked.

She turned, startled. "Oh, I didn't know anybody was there."

Carol's mascara ran down her smoky, blue eyes. She stood there, exposed and hurt as she rubbed her arms. She was short and cute but Sal knew she had zero self-esteem. He had heard most actors were like that.

"Sorry, I was just walking to my truck."

"Oh, ok. Well, I'm fine. Just pondering some life choices."

"Seems to be the theme of the night. Name's Salvador Santos, but you can call me Sal."

"Hey, Sal. So uh, you're the military advisor or something, right? How do you like that?"

"It's ok. It brings in some money, keeps me alive."

"Yeah. That's all of us," she said smiling. "You were in the Marines or something?"

"Army. Just for a short stint. Did see some fighting over in Iraq, though. Nothing too interesting about me. Where you from, Ms. Connors?"

"I'm from Kansas City, Missouri. Nothing too interesting there, either. Which is why I came to California. You know the old story: young girl trying to break into Hollywood. Except I found myself doing these kind of roles over and over again. All it's gotten me is a small apartment just off skid row."

"Consider yourself lucky. See that truck over there?" Sal said pointing to a red pickup a few yards away. She nodded. "That's my home."

"Oh, I'm so sorry. You don't suffer from post-traumatic stress disorder do you?"

"No, ma'am I don't. I suffer from what's called debt. It's the invisible land mine life placed in front of me. Trying to pay it off. So I take whatever gigs I can get. Old buddy suggested movie consultations, and this would be my second so far. But after seeing this production, I think I might just have to donate some of my funds here," he said with a smile.

She smiled back. The spotlight came back on and the four extras came back into position. Jack Grier, the Scorpiosaurus puppeteer, got into the headpiece and began moving it around. The stagehands drew back the wires that controlled the pneumatic tail.

Dino DeLuca waddled to his director's chair as Mike Miller came back with a fresh change of clothes.

"Alright, looks like it's time to finish the scene. Nice talking to you, Sal."

"Likewise."

She wiped her eyes and walked ahead. Sal walked to his truck and checked his phone. No reception. He forgot there would be no service out in the desert. He hoped his weekly check cleared. Some bookies could be quite merciless. He let that sink in for a moment and shivered.

A crew member clapped the slate. The actors spat their bad dialogue. Sal hoped they had taken his advice to heart, though the way the director was running things, he doubted it. For a moment he wondered why he was brought onboard to begin with, but then decided it didn't matter as long as he was getting paid.

The tail struck Mike Miller and lifted him a few inches off the ground. His feet dangled loosely as he opened his mouth to deliver his final line when a large fireball erupted in the distance. The black horizon became engulfed in bright orange light before the boom of thunder rocked the desert.

Sal instinctively hit the floor and rolled under his truck. The crew watched the horizon as they covered their faces from the blinding light.

Sal heard Dino's voice over the blast. "No, keep rolling! We could use this!"

The rattle of distant machinery inched closer. Out in the dark, something heavy rolled ferociously over sand and grime. Sal rolled back up and tried to find the location of the sound. He closed his eyes and listened: north of their location; half a mile now. It sounded like a car.

Carol Connors stepped back as the sound grew nearer. Mike Miller hung helpless from the wires as the stagehands took a few steps back.

Then Sal saw it. A black van barreled out of the darkness and toward the set. The stagehands scrambled to remove the scorpion tail and tried to lower Mike Miller, but it was too late. The van plowed through the soap actor's body like a linebacker through a ballerina. The momentum jerked his harness apart and offered his body to the van.

The body tumbled underneath the wheels as the van skidded, then rolled over and crashed into one of the two generators. The spotlight went dead. The van came to a stop in the middle of the set as Mike Miller's body lay mangled and contorted.

An old man in a white lab coat stumbled out of the van. He looked around as horrified faces stared in confusion. The man grabbed his hair and screamed.

Sal had heard that kind of scream before. Like the wails of a father finding his son killed by a stray bullet, or the screams of a soldier feeling the kick of guilt for his first kill.

The old man ran to Dino and grabbed him by the collar. "You have to get out of here. All of you. You hear me?"

Dino raised his arms in a look of terror. He wasn't used to being accosted.

"You are all dead! Something terrible has happened. Please, go, run!"

Sal rushed to the screaming man and put him in a chokehold. He fought off Sal's attempt and writhed in a maelstrom of kicks and profanities. Sal tightened his grip until the man's body went limp. He then eased the man onto the ground as everyone watched in silence.

Sal bit his lip and felt something kick in he hadn't felt in years: the rush of an emergency. "Do we have a medic on this production?"

A man raised his hand and got the hint. He picked up a first aid kit, ran to Mike, and crouched beside him.

MOTHSQUITO

"Somebody get on the radio and call for emergency services. We are in no position to move Mike's body the way he is."

"That won't matter now," the medic said. "He's dead."

Everything was dead: Mike, one of the generators, even the only radio.

Sal and the medic, Edward Lucas, moved Mike's body into the back of one of the vans. They agreed it was best that Edward drive the 15 miles to the nearest gas station and call for the authorities, while Sal would keep the crazed man subdued.

The crew gathered together in fear and confusion. Carol Connors started to cry as she held Cookie to her chest, though Sal doubted she was attached to Mike all that much; most likely the halt in the production had upset her.

Marty Brenner scribbled some things in his notebook and Sal wondered if he had been taking notes for a future story. Dino DeLuca lit up a cigarette and paced back and forth as he kicked dirt.

Nate and the boys were still in their military duds and had slung their Russian rifles over their shoulders as they chatted away. They looked like kids trying to play soldier.

Jack Grier packed the Scorpiosaurus face and pneumatic tail into a van and hooked up the spotlight to the last generator and adjusted it so the crew wouldn't be blinded.

The old man started to come to. Sal had placed him on the back of his pickup truck. His eyes opened and took a while in registering his situation. Sal let him sit up, but he was ready to pounce if need be. The old man rubbed his neck and shook his head. "Please, listen to me. You must go far away from here. Something terrible is coming."

"Do you know what you've done here?" Sal asked ignoring the last statement.

"I remember driving towards your light. The light! You have to turn off your lights!" The man tried to jump out of the flatbed. Sal held him down. The crew gathered around the commotion.

"You've killed a man!" Sal shouted.

"I had no choice. They would have done the same. They knew the sacrifice…"

"*They*? Who are you?"

"I am Alfonzo Arias, a scientist at the Geitner Air Force Base, ten miles north of this position."

"I've never heard of that base."

Arias gave him a grim look. "Good."

"Tell me what's going on."

"We were working on a biological weapon. An animal hybrid to be exact." We wanted to create an animal that could not only kill enemy combatants, but could also be resourceful, be diurnal and nocturnal; a weapon that could transmute disease and spawn offspring. The perfect living weapon."

"I see," Sal said with a hint of sarcasm. "And what animals did you use in your experiment, Doctor?"

MOTHSQUITO

"We used the nocturnal elements of a moth as well as its ability to form a cocoon to protect its eggs. Another reason is that they are resourceful in that moths can feed off plants and fabrics, resources which can be found virtually anywhere. Then, we took the blood-sucking abilities of a mosquito which as you may well know are vectors of disease. Not only could our creature kill with its sting, but if the target happened to survive the attack, it would be infected with any disease of our engineering, thus becoming a carrier for the disease in turn. We used an Asian tiger mosquito for its diurnal habits. And before we knew it, we had created a killer. A killer we couldn't control. A Mothsquito."

Marty licked his lips and scribbled furiously. This must have been gold for him.

"Couldn't you just spray it or swat it?" asked Carol Connors, holding her trembling dog.

"No, in our concentration, we forgot to plan for a contingency. As for swatting it... we created a ten foot monster."

"What was that explosion?" Jack Grier asked. "You came from that direction. Was that the base?"

Arias lowered his head and clenched his fists. "I had no choice, it broke loose. If it escaped, it could breed indefinitely with no end. I had to stop it, so I destroyed the base. Everyone is gone, and I still failed."

"Wait. Breed with no end? How?" asked Sal. "Wouldn't it need a mate?"

"That's the problem," said Arias. "We made it asexual. Once it feeds, it can begin the asexual reproduction process. It creates its own eggs, encases them in a sturdy cocoon, and once they hatch, the cycle will repeat itself a hundredfold."

"Jesus, you guys are a bunch of sick bastards," Dino DeLuca finally chimed in with a mischievous smile. "Prove it. I'd like to film it."

"Film it? Are you mad? Who the hell are you?"

"You are on my film set, Mr. Arias. And you need to get this Mothsquito here. You did kill my star, it's the least you could do."

"You actually believe him?" Sal asked.

Dino shrugged and took a drag from his cigarette.

"Sal's right. This is crazy," said Carol.

"No, please! You have to believe me. It will only be a matter of time. It will find us. It will be attracted to our sweat, to our scents. And…the light! Turn off your spotlight!" Arias said pointing to the sole blue light that lit the set.

Sal frowned and shook his head. "If it'll quiet you down. Nate, can you get one of your guys to turn that thing off for a moment?"

Nate nodded. "Joe, can you hit that switch over there? Let's humor the good doctor."

Joe walked over to the spotlight as his boots crunched dirt and gravel. As the military extra neared the hot spotlight, he took off his helmet and wiped his sweaty forehead with the back of his hand.

A sharp, thin appendage pierced Joe's tactical vest. A geyser of crimson erupted outward. Joe stared at his belly and the three-foot protrusion. A loud, angry buzz filled the air like the rotors of a helicopter. Joe's body was lifted off the ground as the crew broke out in screams.

Then it materialized out of the dark and into the spotlight. It had the face of a mosquito with large antennae that moved about like feelers. It had round, compound eyes staring off into unseen directions. Its thorax was a lumpy, furry mass, like that of a moth. The fur rippled in waves as a warm current of desert air blew in. Six long legs wrapped around Joe like fingers around a knife. Its long abdomen hung close to the ground in multiple yellow segments as blood dripped down its length and pooled on the floor. It spread two large, furry wings with a series of organic and geometric patterns. As the wings flapped together, the Mothsquito thrust upwards and created a powerful current of cool air, like an industrial fan.

In what must have been instinct, Joe yelled, drew his rifle, and fired at nothing in particular as he was hauled off behind the shroud of night. The muzzle fire faded a few moments later and gave way to silence.

Two of the stagehands panicked and broke for the desert. Sal made a move to chase after them but stopped himself. Their howls echoed deep into the darkness and eventually disappeared.

"Damn," he muttered under his breath.

"What the fuck was that?" shouted Jack.

"It's the Mothsquito!" shouted Arias.

"Someone, turn on the cameras before it comes for another pass," Dino yelled.

"No! The moth's features draw it to bright lights. Someone has to turn the light off."

"No way. You saw what happened to Joe," Nate said as he gripped his rifle, looking around him. Sal hoped Nate remembered it fired blanks.

"Fine, I'll do it," Sal said with a sigh. He broke into a sprint. The warm desert breeze flowed through his hair as he sped through the bodies frozen in fear. He stepped on a pool of Joe's blood and nearly slipped on the mush it had made of the ground. He tagged the off switch and shoulder rolled forward in anticipation of anything in the shadows.

Nothing happened, and only the sound of a subtle wind blowing through the Joshua trees and dry brush could be heard. Sal backed into the crew. They had instinctively huddled together by his truck at the center of the production set. Sal did a quick head count: Carol, Dino, Marty, Arias, Jack, Nate and two other extras whose names he'd forgotten.

"Okay, Doc, what the hell do we do now?" Sal asked with a piercing tone.

"I don't know," Arias said running a hand through his silver hair. "I don't know."

"Well, tell us more about this damn thing. What are its next steps?"

"It will continue to feed until it has enough sustenance to lay its eggs. Then it will lay them in a cocoon close to a body of water."

"Wait," said Marty putting down his notebook. "There aren't any significant bodies of water around here."

"Correct. Once it is done with us, it will travel to more populated areas and stage a breeding ground there. Which is why we are now, regrettably, the last line of defense before it reaches the rest of humanity."

"Jesus," Nate said pulling his Ak-47 to his chest like a scared man heading for battle.

"So you're saying this Mothsquito is gonna pick us off until it's sucked us dry?" Sal asked.

Arias nodded his head and looked down.

Carol trembled as she held her dog close. "I'm going to my trailer. You are all welcome to come inside. I mean, we can't just stand out here, right?"

"No, it is attracted to heat as well. In moments your trailer will become warmer and warmer until it has found us and trapped us all inside. Its mandibles can tear through thin layers of metal."

"You really did your homework didn't you? What the hell were you thinking tampering with nature like that?" Sal asked. "There has to be a way of killing it."

"We wanted to create a weapon that needed no supervision. Something we could drop on our enemy's doorstep and forget about. We are all on its dinner plate. The only way to kill it is just how you kill everything else."

Sal raised an eyebrow.

"Excessive force," said Arias.

"Well then, we are truly screwed, my friend," said Dino as he lit another cigarette. Sweat started to soak through his Hawaiian shirt. "All we have are silly props and cameras. All we can shoot is film, not bullets."

Nate looked at his rifle and eased his grip. The other men did the same as the feeling of safety slipped through their hands.

"This isn't happening," Carol said as tears trickled down her cheek. "It's like a bad horror film. Can't we just drive away and look for help?"

"This project is off the books. No one would believe me until it is too late. We *have* to stop this. Besides, with all the noise and heat exhaust from a car, it would track you down and dismantle you in moments."

Dino shook his head and began pacing back and forth. He was getting anxious. Sal knew the look. He had learned not to trust someone with that look shortly before battle. Their nerves always got a hold of their common sense; someone like that was always unpredictable.

"Screw it, I'm going to turn the camera on," Dino said as he waddled away. "This is going to make me rich."

"No, Dino, wait. The camera produces heat!" Jack shouted.

Dino flipped the camera switch. He hunched over the camera as sweat soaked through his back. He looked through the viewfinder and played with the focus. A loud flap filled the air and a gust of wind lifted his shirt. A large, barbed leg came into focus. Dino smiled and panned back for a wide shot. It hovered above the Italian director like a chopper in an extraction mission. It must have been ten to twelve feet long, with legs just as big. Its wingspan must have been double that.

Mothsquito swiped at the camera and knocked it down. Dino raised his arms in anger and threw his cap at the monster. "You idiot!" he shouted.

The flying monster wrapped its forelegs around Dino's fat neck and pulled his head straight off. It inserted its stinger down Dino's gaping neck wound and produced loud slurping noises.

Carol moaned and fell to the floor. Cookie barked and ran under the monster's legs. Nate whipped his rifle upwards, stared down the sights, and engaged the Mothsquito, full-auto. At least he had gotten one of the steps right. The two other men followed his queue and did the same. The shots cracked like popcorn as Mothsquito turned to the military extras. Dino's body slumped to the floor as Mothsquito flapped its wings. Cookie jumped up and nipped the creature's leg. Its mandibles clicked and made a high-pitched whine. The Chihuahua ran away and hid under Sal's truck.

As Mothsquito lifted off the ground, Sal picked up Carol and tossed her over his shoulder. He placed her on his flatbed, next to Arias, who watched the unfolding horror in awe of his creation in action.

The three extras fired an onslaught of blanks in an absurd stroke of reasoning. Mothsquito hovered towards the flashing lights, mandibles snapping.

"Damnit, Nate, stop firing!" Sal said.

They couldn't hear him over the automatic fire. Mothsquito stabbed Nate in the leg with its stinger. He dropped and grabbed his bleeding limb in shrieks of agony. One of the other extras ran out of ammo and swung his rifle like a club. The insect monstrosity leaned its head into the brave extra's face and snapped its mandibles shut. His skull collapsed inwards in a burst of blood. The third extra shot a barrage of blanks into the creature's eye. It shrieked and swung a leg, hurling the man head-first into Carol's trailer.

Marty ran to Sal. His eyes were glassy and had bags underneath them. "Sal, it's all over, man."

"Marty, have you been smoking again?"

He nodded and smiled. The first time Sal had seen him do so. "I'm writing my own ticket out of this one. This movie would've been perfect if we could pit Scorpiosaurus against Mothsquito. It would be our only chance. Just like the movies: monster versus monster. Unfortunately, it's a story that'll never be told."

Marty pulled out his pen and sprinted toward Mothsquito. Marty drew his hand back and leapt in the air. The bug turned and caught the writer with its legs. It flew upwards and held Marty in a snug embrace and pulled apart his torso, raining blood and guts on the set.

Sal bit his lip and hoped Marty's pain was now truly over.

Mothsquito landed and began feeding on the rest of Dino's headless corpse.

"Jesus," said Jack Grier. He looked away and saw Nate in a pool of his own blood. "Fuck. Sal, over here," he said pointing to Nate. "He's bleeding out."

"No, stay away from him," yelled Arias. "He has been infected with the bubonic plague."

"You're kidding me," said Jack as he backed away from Nate.

Nate grimaced and pulled himself forward. "Help me," he said looking at Jack.

"Stay away from him!" Arias shouted.

MOTHSQUITO

Jack shook his head and ran to Nate. "We're all dead anyway. I can't leave him like this." Jack pulled Nate upwards and slung his arm over his neck. The two limped over to Carol's trailer. Jack helped him up the steps and placed him on Carol's bed. "Stay here. We'll be back for you."

Jack ran back to Sal's truck. "Is this okay? I mean, he didn't cough on me or anything…"

"Yeah, it's alright. Like you said, if we don't figure something out, we're all dead anyway." Sal looked at the old man and grabbed him by the collar. "Damnit man, how are we supposed to stop this thing? This isn't some shitty movie, where I pull a flare strapped to a pipe bomb out of my ass or something."

The old man said nothing.

Carol stirred. She moaned and reached out an arm. "Where's Cookie?"

Cookie yapped from under Sal's truck. He let go of Arias, picked it up and handed her the dog. She squeezed him and said, "Oh, Cookie. If only you were big enough to take on that bug."

Sal looked at his feet and furrowed his brows. The thought burrowed into his mind. Why didn't he think of it before? "That's it. Damnit, that's it."

"What, Sal? What's it?" asked Jack.

"Marty had the right idea, though he was thinking movie," Sal said. He shook his head, "Anyway, we don't have any weapons but we do have something powerful enough to kill it. And a means to lure it."

"Well, spit it out man," Jack said irritated.

"We're going to lure it with the spotlight. And then, we're going to kill it with our own monster.

Jack, I need you to help me load a few things onto my pickup."

"Sal, are you thinking what I think you're thinking?"

"Yes. Damnit, Jack, it's our only shot."

"Right. Okay. Okay. You're right. Well, let's get a move on."

"Carol," Sal said. "Take Cookie and Doctor Arias and follow me to the van. When we get there, I want you all to be quiet and stay inside. Let's move."

They ran to the van and swung the doors open. Jack escorted Carol and Arias inside. Sal checked on the Mothsquito; it had moved on to feasting on the dead extra outside the trailer. Its stinger was deep into the kid's chest. He hoped it didn't pick up Nate's scent.

They lugged the pneumatic Scorpiosaurus tail and its switchbox onto the back of the flatbed. It was heavy. Sal remembered lugging around some heavy gear in the army but this was worse. This was raw; this was survival and he was outmatched. But when the ammo dried up, you always fought back with your wits.

They hauled the spotlight and moved it to the front of the flatbed.

Jack wheeled the generator to the truck. "There's no room for the generator," he whispered.

Sal opened the passenger side door. Jack smiled and together they lifted it onto the seat and secured it with a seat belt. They connected all the wiring and started it up. It rumbled to life like a lawnmower.

MOTHSQUITO

Mothsquito abandoned the dead soldier and moved its antennae through the air. It was feeling for its next meal.

"Jack, I'm gonna need you to drive."

"Don't tell me you're gonna go back there? Let me do it. I know how to operate the controls."

"No, it was my idea. I can't ask you to risk it. Just tell me what to do."

Jack handed him the control switch which was wired to the base of the tail. "Push this button and the tail shoots out in an overhead hooking motion. You know, like a scorpion. Make sure to be out of its way. It's highly pressurized and launches at speeds of about a hundred feet per second. The light you already know how to turn on."

Sal nodded and hugged Jack. "It's been great knowing you."

"Likewise," said Jack Grier as he hopped in the truck and started the ignition. Mothsquito turned its head toward the pickup. Sal eyed Nate's rifle and scooped it up. He leaped onto the back of the truck and knocked on the driver side door. Jack hit the gas.

Sal aimed the rifle at the creature's eye and cracked off a shot. The bug shrieked and flapped its wings. The truck picked up speed as the set became smaller and smaller in the distance.

Sal hit a switch and the spotlight came on. Mothsquito came into full, detailed view. A gang of long, barbed legs hovered in the sky. The sound of its mandibles could be heard as they snapped open and shut. Sal had been nervous before; hell, he had fought other armed men. But they knew fear too. This monstrosity felt nothing but an insatiable lust for blood. Never had he encountered something so grotesque, so paralyzing. He found his hand trembling on the switch.

Mothsquito flapped its wings faster now; its hypnotizing designs came alive in the light's blue glow. Green swirls and black splotches stared back at him. They were almost beautiful. He shook his head and focused. Mothsquito was nearly aligned with the back of the truck. It bounced up and down as the wheels ran through cracks and small rocks.

Damnit, Jack, keep it steady.

The creature's stinger came into focus. It was pointed, sharp. Sal had no trouble imagining it piercing his heart.

Its forelegs latched on to the tip of the flatbed, tipping the truck downward. The back wheels started grinding violently against the desert floor.

"Shit," said Sal.

Mothsquito brought its other legs forward and anchored them to the bed. Its wings stopped flapping as it let out a loud hiss and lurched forward. The extra weight pressed the truck down so that the front tipped upward completely. A tire popped. The truck bumped and skidded sideways, sending the switchbox over the edge of the bed.

"Fuck," Sal said under his breath.

The switchbox was being dragged on the ground, just under Mothsquito's body.

The creature's face was now three feet away from Sal's as it snapped its mandibles at the spotlight. Its forelegs slashed at the light, cracking the glass.

MOTHSQUITO

He could see the button just over the edge of the truck. The box sent sparks flying upwards. The switch's cable was starting to wear as the protective rubber tore apart strand by strand. There was no way to make a grab at it without being directly underneath the monster.

But, there was one way; maybe if he could shoot the button...

He raised the Ak-47 and looked down the sights. The flat tire made the ride unsteady as the truck bumped up and down. He fired a shot – miss.

Mothsquito cracked the spotlight. Glass blew upward as the light died.

He fired another shot – another miss.

Mothsquito crawled on top of the broken spotlight. Its face lit only by the moonlight now, but its terrible features still visible. It aimed its stinger at Sal's throat.

He held his breath and aimed down the sight. He squeezed the trigger.

A loud hiss of compressed air erupted outward, followed by a loud snap. A mechanical whir droned overhead and a sharp, seven foot tail lashed downwards, impaling Mothsquito's head, burying itself into the flatbed. A splatter of green goop flew everywhere. The creature writhed as it threw its legs about and spread its wings. After a while, it stopped moving and the wings collapsed into themselves.

Sal leaned back and took a breath. He tapped the cab window. Jack stopped the truck and got out.

Jack looked at the monster's body, as the wind rippled through its furry thorax.

"Holy shit, Sal. We did it?"

"We did it," Sal said as he dropped the rifle. He tapped the pneumatic tail. "Thank Scorpiosaurus."

"What a nightmare that was," Jack said taking a deep breath.

"Yeah. I'm never doing another movie again." Sal pulled out a pack of cigarettes and lit one up. "Just hope my check cleared."

The first signs of dawn broke through the horizon. In the distance, he could make out the vans and trailers of the set. It was a long walk back, but Sal had marched for many miles in the Army.

"Long way back. Think you're up for it?"

Jack nodded his head. "Yeah. After tonight, this should be a piece of cake. Besides, Nate needs help, and we need to have a stern chat with the good doctor."

They trekked across the desert, swatting away small gnats and mosquitoes.

"Think we can salvage any of that film?" Jack asked with a wicked grin.

Sal smiled. "Maybe."

"Think it'll make us money?"

Sal had seen enough B-films to know that answer. "Hell no."

They laughed and watched the first glimmers of a new sunrise.

DIPPEL'S MONKEY
by Gordon Grice

The evidence was plain. The soul had something to do with that elusive force called galvanism, the very force that had kissed and bitten his fingers when he stacked the metal plates in jars of salty water. It lingered in the human body a day or so past death. This surely was his road to fame. No more would Dippel work to turn flecks of mica into gold or generate a human fetus from moldering hay. The next step was obvious. He would confirm his theory by catching a soul before it could escape. He would plant it in some other body. It couldn't be a human body, obviously, because that would already have a soul in it. But animals don't have souls, so—

"But I've always felt animals do have souls, Joseph," Dippel's mother said as he tried to explain his theory over scones and marmalade one morning.

"Especially horses," said his sister Mina. "You can see it in their eyes." She lowered her gaze to the cup of tea between her pale hands, as if imagining a mahogany eye in it.

"I'm hardly likely to plant a human soul in the body of a horse," Dippel said, trying to hide his irritation. "It would be too cruel. Imagine a man returned from death, but unable to tell us of his experiences. No, the receptacle must resemble the human."

So his mother and sister weren't surprised when he returned from Grotz with a monkey. It cringed in its poultry crate, peering between the slats. When Dippel pried the crate open, it cowered in a corner and screamed like a child, the pointed tufts in its ears twitching.

"Why doesn't he come out?" Dippel said.

"He thinks we'll hurt him," Mina said. "Who knows what sort of people he's met before?"

It was a day or so before the monkey would show itself without scampering under a cupboard. Mina was delighted. She soon had the little fellow leaping to catch chestnuts. It chafed them between its palms, then peeled them with its side-teeth.

"I worry about her, Joseph," Madame Dippel said. "She ought to be married by now, but she sits playing like a child."

"Leave her be, Mama," Dippel said. "She's only lonely."

Perhaps, he thought, the monkey would make a better companion when he'd finished his work—someone who could not merely play with his lonely sister, but converse. The thought made him uncomfortable. The monkey, so maddeningly human in the movements of its hands, in the clarity of its moods, nonetheless revealed its animal nature daily. It sat fingering lice and nits from its fur and then sucking them, with squeaks of pleasure, down through the gap between bucked incisor and fang.

DIPPEL'S MONKEY

Mina kissed the monkey, who recoiled only slightly. "He's delightful, Joseph!" she said. "I'll name him—" but it was ridiculous to name a bit of experimental material, and Dippel quietly refused to join his family in the practice.

One day Dippel showed them the device he'd been working on, a funnel-shaped affair with complicated grooves inside.

"I call it the Soul-Sifter," he announced. "I insert it surgically, then pour in a purified slurry made from the brain of someone recently dead."

"Surgery?" Mina said. "You mean cutting? But he hasn't done anything to deserve that!"

"Not to worry, darling," Dippel said. "Animals don't feel pain the way we do. Their reactions are mere reflex."

"But a human brain?" Madame Dippel said. Her look shriveled him. He'd seen it before—her suspicion that her son was doing something disreputable. He'd tried to explain how his work might reveal layers of God's creation none had ever noticed before, but every explanation seemed to deepen her suspicion.

"Don't worry, Mama," he said now. "The Church approves such study these days. What I propose does not involve us in sin." He wondered whether his tone was quite convincing.

The following morning Mina and Madame Dippel set out to visit Uncle Friedrich on the far side of the mountain. An overdue visit, his mother said, but Dippel knew disapproval was at its root.

"Don't cry, Mina," Dippel said. "I'll take care to spare him pain." But Mina turned away on the carriage seat and said nothing. The monkey sat on

Dippel's shoulder, fingering among his fair curls for lice, its back rounded exactly the way Mina's was. The driver clucked to the horses. Mina kept her back to her brother as the carriage lumbered out of sight.

A human brain, indeed. The question of how to find one in the proper state troubled Dippel as much as it did his mother. No one had lately died in his country neighborhood. The answer came like a gift from God, in the form of the garrulous old peddler who passed this way once or twice a year. Always he was full of gossip from the capital, and fuller still of drink. Dippel had noted the signs of his decline when he stayed with them the fall before—the blood vessels threading more and more visibly down his swollen cheeks, the gouty walk, the way he refused a dish of cream because of his digestion. Dippel had even mentioned it to his mother at the time.

"Perhaps we can take him on as a stable hand—Jorgis could use the help anyway—so that when he dies someone will be at hand to bury him as a Christian," he'd said. And his mother had patted his arm.

"You're a generous boy, Joseph, but the truth is, I've already told Jorgis he'll have to find a new situation," she said. She went on to remind him times were hard for a family of displaced nobles; and besides, the old peddler had a reputation for saying things he shouldn't in front of people's daughters.

And now here he was, coming along the road with a gait goutier than ever, his back crooked under his peddler's bag, singing his wares in a voice more broken than before.

It would be a gift to the old man. It would be a lifting of his burden. It would give him a role in the revelation of God's works.

Still, Dippel went out among the oaks and told his rosary and paused, fingering the black beads, until he felt he'd heard his answer in the lightening of his mood.

And so, after quietly visiting his room and pocketing a stoppered bottle from the table where he kept his tinctures, he served supper with his own hands; and if the peddler's portion of barley soup had a certain tinge of blue, he never seemed to notice. "It's good," he said, dabbing at his lips. "Is there, by chance, more?"

Rings of white fur around its eyes made the monkey always seem surprised. It seemed more so when it gulped the brandy Dippel set before it. After the second dose it learned to hold the glass out in its furry hand, asking for more. After the fifth, it ran a circuit of the highest shelves, hurling baskets and buckets, hooting and hissing, showing its differentiated array of teeth—like a wolf's, but with proportionally longer fangs.

Nonetheless, the drink served its purpose. Soon the monkey was snoring like a phlegmatic child as Dippel bound its hands with a belt and shaved its scalp. He paused with the drill in his hand; he'd thought of his sister's face and felt guilty. One translucent pink eyelid flickered. He had to think ahead, to the good a companion could do for

Mina, to the godly end his science might effect. Time was running out; the peddler's soul would disperse soon. Besides, the afternoon sun provided the best light for the kitchen table, as he knew from past experiments, and already the rays were slanting more than he liked. He steeled himself.

The frontal lobe of the peddler's brain sloshed in a pitcher beside him, rocked by his exertions with the drill and awl. It looked like curds bobbing atop the whey.

The monkey shivered for half an hour before it woke. Dippel feared the seizures would kill it, but finally its pink eyelids flickered open. The eyes gazed irritably at nothing. It repeated the process of sleeping, shivering, and waking. Dippel grew impatient and used the time to bury a certain burden in the woods, just off the path to the spring in a spot hidden among rotting logs. It seemed egregious that the black flies kept nibbling at his neck and wrists, ignoring the corpse whose blood was going to waste anyway.

When he entered the house again, the monkey was awake, its eyes flitting to the candle he'd lit against the evening, and then away again, its expression one of extreme irritation.

"Those black flies would have given you something to be angry about," Dippel said, washing his hands and neck at the sink. The black flies had left him dotted with blood that smeared his towel. The monkey only looked at him with irritation. Except for its eyes, it made no movement.

Dippel was impatient to see how it would act, for how else could he know if the operation had succeeded? But the monkey closed its eyes with elaborate slowness and began to snore. Dippel suddenly felt himself sleepy as well. He washed his hands again—unnecessarily, perhaps, but he seemed to smell brandy and blood on them still.

When he woke, the sun was high; he must have slept through the night and well into the morning beyond. The candle was a hardened puddle on the table. The monkey was looking at him from under a puzzled brow. He loosed the belt from its hands. It examined the hands as if it had never seen them before.

"You might say hello," Dippel suggested. He felt foolish talking to an animal—for in the morning light his entire experiment seemed improbable, and the monkey only a monkey, bald and wounded though it was.

Presently, however, it crossed its arms and began to survey the room with a skeptical air.

"I believe you do understand me," Dippel said.

The monkey tried to rise, then collapsed into a convulsion, like a shot dog.

Later, as he pored over his anatomy manual by candlelight, Dippel glimpsed a shadowy motion in the clutter of the kitchen table. It was the monkey, pawing among the plates. He hadn't seen it move for hours, but here it was, not four feet from him, alert, mobile, showing fine motor control as it picked up a fork, then a salt cellar, then, alarmingly, a knife—and put them aside. It found, at last, what it was looking for: the glass he'd served the brandy in. It gazed into the empty glass, looked puzzled, reached inside. He saw its fingertips flatten against the bottom like dollops of dough. It pulled the hand out and licked each finger pad in slow succession.

For a while it refused all nourishment except the sips of brandy Dippel allowed. It answered his questions only with a melancholy gaze. Eventually, however, when he set a plate of stewed pork and apple slivers before it, it tossed the fork and spoon aside, gobbled the food, and held out the plate for more.

The days went on—the monkey silent, but an excellent eater. It grew faster than any organism Dippel had ever encountered except the mushrooms of the woods. It was like the mana the Lord fed the Hebrews in the desert. That, at least, was an interesting result, something to show for his work even if the human soul never showed its presence in the monkey's hollow eyes. Soon it was sitting at the table opposite him at every meal—not on the table, as before, but in a chair, its tail wrapped around one chair leg like a serpent, its hands reaching for food before Dippel could set it down. Nor did barley and oats satisfy; it tossed the tin bowls aside when it found them meatless. Dippel began to think of venturing to the market for a side of beef.

DIPPEL'S MONKEY

"What will Mama say about these accounts?" he asked.

The monkey merely gazed and nibbled its thumb.

One day the monkey finished the stewed pork and prunes Dippel gave it for lunch and held out its plate for more, as usual.

"The pot's empty," Dippel said.

The monkey thrust the tin plate at him and mimicked the movement of ladling food.

"It doesn't matter how often you ask, fool," said Dippel. "The pot is empty." He upended the pot to illustrate.

The monkey grunted and banged the plate on the table.

"Go to your cage!" Dippel said and felt absurd, for the monkey couldn't possibly fit in that flimsy poultry-crate, and hadn't tried for weeks.

The monkey grunted louder, hurled the tin plate, and curled its lips back to show its fangs with their cuffs of yellow calculus.

"You haven't any humanity at all," Dippel said. "I wish I'd never brought you here." He reached for his table knife, for the monkey's mood seemed to darken further at his words.

Suddenly he was on the floor, the table knocked aside, the clatter of dishes and breaking glass in his ears. He'd hardly seen the monkey move. How could it have grown so strong? A strange sensation in his calf intruded, distracted him. He looked, but did not understand. It seemed as if the monkey's head and hands had fallen off; they lay on his leg, the head grinning like a jack-o-lantern. Had there been an explosion? Perhaps he hadn't put his tinctures away securely?

But no; the creature hadn't broken apart, but was merely crouched in a position he'd never seen, like a cat bellying under a fence, and its hands held his leg, the slender fingers adjusting their grip, like spiders running up and down his shin—but the mouth! Its fangs were in his leg, had punctured his trousers and were red all the way up to the yellow calculus. The jaws were big as a man's, though not quite wide enough to snap his tibia.

It was odd, how things moved like molasses. He realized, with a dreamy clarity, that shock was to blame. He saw his own hand moving, with agonizing slowness, toward the monkey's head. He was surprised to see that it contained a knife, for although he now remembered groping for one, he didn't remember to have reached it. The knife made a meaty *chuch* when it punctured the monkey's eye, and then time resumed and everything was red motion.

He found himself seated against the wall, tying a napkin round his leg to stop the blood. The monkey sat in the far corner, gazing at him through its one good eye like tarnished bronze, chewing hungrily at something big as a fist. He wondered what the something was, and then, as if he had arrived at the solution of an equation, realized at least that much flesh was missing from his leg.

DIPPEL'S MONKEY

The blood mopped up easily enough. It was the blue stain on the floor he couldn't get out, made by the cauterizing tincture that pooled beneath him as he worked on his leg.

"It's a good thing I understand medicine," he said, though there was no one, not even the monkey, to hear him. It had stood on its hind legs and walked out the door after it finished its grisly meal, hardly glancing at him again.

The leg seemed safe. He felt confident he wouldn't have to amputate, though he couldn't stop fretting about the saw and how he might position it. A week remained before his mother and sister should return. He might manage to dress himself by then and thus conceal the bandages, with their red and blue stains. Perhaps he could even walk and smile and tell them the limp was a trivial thing. His mother would give him that shriveling gaze, of course, and Mina would want to help. He could put them off. But the stains! Not just the blue on the floor, but the fingerprints he seemed to leave on everything he touched. Given its toxic properties, he would have to make another attempt at washing the blue from the dishes, at least. It was mainly the blue he worried about.

That and the monkey. It might come back.

It must have found something to eat, Dippel thought, for the gray whiskers of its chin were clotted with dark red. He woke slowly, expecting the face at the window to vanish. Surely it was a dream, for the monkey had never been this big. Surely his wound was giving him a fever, making his dreams lurid and swollen. Its brows beetled; you could fit a fist into each of those eye sockets. The candle on the table blazed up a bit and illuminated the bronze good eye.

Dippel tried to hold still. He looked to the door and was relieved to see the bolt still in place. The candle was far from his cot; possibly he was invisible in his corner. He half-closed his eyes: leave nothing for it to see. The window must be too narrow for those shoulders. The restless bronze eye fell upon him then. It looked him up and down, appraising, hungry. He felt ashamed, somehow, of his wound. He didn't want it seen, though of course the monkey already knew all about it.

All the limping way to the well he kept glancing over his shoulder and pausing to peer under bushes. The monkey was nowhere to be seen, but tracks like swollen handprints ran everywhere—beneath each window, in and out of the stable and the privy. At the well he stood working the pump, and suddenly it occurred to him to look up. The trees, of course, leaned everywhere—over the well, even over the house. He saw its face then, gazing at him from the fork of an elm, the good eye open, the ruined one clenched like a fist. He clutched his axe and edged toward the house. The movement, however, made him see that it was no face at all, merely the rugose pattern of the bark.

DIPPEL'S MONKEY

He resolved to be braver. Still, and despite his limp, he couldn't keep himself from rushing back to the house.

He'd reached the door before he saw the mess near the road. Rags, perhaps, or a beggar's bundle come undone. Perhaps it could be ignored. Nevertheless, he moved toward it—by small steps, dragging the bad leg after the good. His feet in the dead leaves made too much noise, he felt; his axe, as he leaned upon it, only made more. Nonetheless. . .

It was clothes, among other things. An apron; a skirt. The small intestine was strung for at least two yards through the grass and weeds.

He ran. He felt his sutures tear, but he ran. He saw the face, again and again, in every tree and even, as he fell, in the dirt, in the seconds before he reached the door. Inside, he shot the bolt and slumped against the door moaning.

Not everything he'd seen was real, he knew. Probably he had not seen the monkey at all. One's nerves; the recent loss of blood.

The things he'd seen near the road, however, were real enough. The smell testified to that. He even recognized the face—a neighbor's girl, hardly ten

He had plenty to do in the hours before dark. First of all, suturing his leg all over again. The pain swelled like a melon, wider than the leg itself.

Second, loading the old musket.

(Someone would come along and see the child, sooner or later. He thought of it with shame, more than anything else. If he were still alive by then, they would ask questions. He would have to admit what an arrogant fool he'd been. He'd have to tell it all, and then he'd get from everyone the shriveling look his mother gave.)

Third, sharpening a knife and wiping a little blue poison along its blade.

(But that wasn't the worst. Madame and Mina would be coming home soon—who knew exactly when, for he'd lost track of the days, and their intentions had been loose to begin with.)

Fourth, and most important, cooking. The last of the pork-side, with savory spices to mask the taste of the blue tincture. Simmer it from the bone.

(Imagine Mina meeting her friend in the woods.)

He watched from the window. The plates he'd heaped with stew sat on the chopping block in the yard, drawing flies. A squirrel with tufted ears frisked in the clearing, paused as if in alarm, bolted. What had it heard? Nothing, nothing Dippel could hear. Once he was startled by an itch and a dripping sound: his bandages were soaked through. Had he fallen asleep, then? For surely he would have noticed before it reached this messy state.

The light declined. All the better; the monkey wouldn't see the blue tinge of the food. But maybe the piling hours only meant it had left the neighborhood, and was even now killing children somewhere else. Or had gone off into the wild to die, to trouble him no more. Some day he would hear of a curious skeleton found in the woods.

Or maybe it was watching the house even now.

When it stepped from the dusky woods, he took it for another fearful hallucination. It was too big, a foot taller than the last time he'd seen it. Its head had grown the most; its great beetling brows made it look like a stone statue. It walked on two feet, like a man, hardly stooping. Its python tail spasmed as it walked; it seemed a separate organism.

It rushed upon the bait, slavering. Dippel took some comfort from that: perhaps it hadn't fed elsewhere. It scooped food with both hands, shoving it in. Relief flooded Dippel's soul. He held still. Let no motion of his disturb the creature at its feast.

Abruptly the monkey spat out the food. It dug with its hairy-knuckled fists in its mouth, scraping every morsel out. Whines of protest—Dippel felt sorry for it. How curious that its voice had not grown with its stature. It bent over and vomited into the grass, great red masses, bright even in the failing light. This, clearly, was food it had eaten elsewhere. It whined piteously. Then it looked up—straight into Dippel's eyes.

This time he wasn't surprised at its speed. It seemed natural that the hairy hands were at his throat before he heard the window shatter. The window frame tilted, came toward him. There was blood in the fur of its chest, in the gray fringe round its eyes. The eye he had stabbed pouted like pursed lips—like his mother's lips, in fact, when she gave him the shriveling look.

Everything was slow again. He wondered, without hurry, which of his vessels the great teeth had punctured. Not the carotid, surely, for though there was blood, he did not lose consciousness. The big hands tore his shirt away, then his trousers. It was a bit embarrassing. When the beast reared its head to smile at him, the bright arterial blood rilled through its teeth. It was wonderful, really, how the liquid looked like braided twine, then flattened into the foliations of the creature's skin. Even the dance of blood revealed God's geometry. It was all languidly fascinating.

The distressing part was the hooves and carriage wheels he heard. That meant his mother and Mina were nearly home. Unless it was someone else. His mother would disapprove of the way he'd kept house. Mina would be surprised how her little friend had grown. He heard the wheels slow, and the whinny as the driver turned the horse into their yard. The monkey cocked its head, hearing it too.

SLOTH ZOMBIES
by The Frightening Floyds

Voodoo Vicky's was little more than a shack on the outskirts of town. To the paranormal enthusiasts, it was the premier metaphysical shop, and Vicky herself was rumored to be an adept practitioner of voodoo and hoodoo conjure. Visitors frequented her shop for protection spells, charms, and other aspects of the art *and* religion; then there were those who sought out her hoodoo powers – for the darker requests, in which Vicky was particularly skilled. The dark side of hoodoo was her primary focus, because Vicky had hate in her heart.

The young lady was hateful for good reason, too. Those who were not enthused by the paranormal thought of her in the typical way regular God-fearing, small-town folk thought of such people: they proclaimed she was a freak, witch, weirdo, and Satanist. Though she did not deny these claims, she didn't appreciate the accompanying scorn. This hate had grown over many years of mistreatment, dating back to her childhood, when she was given the moniker 'Voodoo Vicky'. The exact events that led to this nickname eluded her; it might have been when she brought her tarantula to school for show-and-tell;

or it could have been because she always wore black with heavy metal and punk band tee shirts.

Vicky was a goth and she received all the expected sneers and torment from the "regular people". Yes – the torment is what got her into witchcraft, cursing, and conjuring. Her work was a combination of hoodoo and theistic Satanism, and it was her craving for more than mere vengeance that drew her to such a dark and powerful combination – it was her desire to harm many people at once, and to gain the ability to maintain the suffering for as long as she wished. Vicky traded everything she had for this power, but she had to wait until she could unleash it; however, once she did, it was hers to use whenever she saw fit.

Of course, this edict came from the Dark Lord himself. "Wait until the first full moon of your thirtieth year, for three mocks the Holy Trinity. Prepare yourself well, for on that night you will be blessed by both Lilith and Hekate and permitted to unleash your fury."

And, as you might have guessed, this story takes place on that very night.

Vicky locked her shop door and turned the 'closed' sign around. Normally, she was open from 3pm until 3am. Today, she had special hours—3pm to 6pm—so she could prepare for her revenge.

Papa Legba stood by the counter, shaking dust off his straw hat and brushing his long, mighty beard. "Are you sure you want to do this, girl?"

SLOTH ZOMBIES

"I've never been surer of anything."

"Oh dear." Papa Legba placed the hat back on his head. "You are at a real crossroads."

"That's why you're here, isn't it?" Vicky grabbed a handful of leaves and bits of a chopped-up peach.

Papa Legba straightened. "Is that for me?"

"No. But there is a basket of fruit and some turkey under the counter."

The ancient loa grinned and rubbed his hands together. "Oh child, you know how to please old Papa Legba."

While Papa was retrieving the offering, Vicky stopped at a seven-by-seven-foot cage containing four young sloths, and sprinkled the leaves and peach bits around for them. They immediately began dragging themselves to dinner.

When she closed the cage and turned, Papa was devouring the turkey. "You sure make some good smoked turkey, girl."

Vicky waved the comment off. "It's easy."

Returning to the counter, she pulled her chair out and sat down. There was a box under the counter full of apples and raw meat. Papa Legba sniffed the air. "Is that chicken?"

"Yes. I would have prepared it for you, but I need to give it to *them*."

"Oh," he said slowly and in a low tone. "I see."

Vicky gave a weak smile and plopped the box on the counter. "It's their encouragement, I suppose. Besides, it's part of the incantation."

Papa Legba put down a peach he was eating and cleared his throat.

"Oh boy," Vicky said. "Here it comes."

THE FRIGHTENING FLOYDS

"Now don't be like that, child. You should listen to Papa Legba. He's been around for a while."

Grabbing a nail file then filing her nails nervously, Vicky blew back strands of her curly black hair and said, "I know it's going to be serious when you use third person."

Papa sighed. "You meddle in bad things. The words the Devil says, they aren't always the definitions you believe."

"I've dealt with him before, Papa. I know."

"Yes, yes. I know you have. But you never did anything like this. This is bad juju."

Vicky stopped filing and looked up at him, pursing her lips to the left and raising her eyebrows. "Is it? I mean, is it not what they deserve?"

"Now dear, have any of them hurt you so bad?"

"Yes. They've ruined my life. I practically live in the woods because I can't stay in town without being harassed."

"I know dear. But why not try to make them see reason? Use your skills for that."

"You think I never have?"

"I know you have."

Vicky held out her hands and Papa Legba nodded.

"So, I guess there's no changing your mind?"

"Nope."

"What if I told you about the karma you'd be bringing on yourself?"

"I'd tell you I don't care. My life already sucks enough. I say bring it on, karma."

SLOTH ZOMBIES

Papa went back to his basket. "It is a most unfortunate thing that it has come to this. Did you really have to ask the Devil for help?"

"Why not?"

"He's got such bad intentions."

"So do I. The Devil understands being stabbed in the back and kicked out of town. Who better to ask than one of the most misunderstood beings in the history of human existence?"

"But he is no human."

"But he knows us well. Better than we know ourselves; and, he can get the job done."

"But taking on his power…once you let that in, it never leaves. You'll carry a piece of him around for eternity."

"Thanks for your concern, Papa. But I'm a big girl – I can handle myself."

"Yes child, I know. You are stronger than you know – too strong to have to ask the Devil for help."

"I just want to make sure the process is as seamless as possible."

"You don't need Ol' Scratch's help for that; you just need more confidence in your own abilities."

Vicky made a face and smiled, then looked towards the door. It was evening time in winter, so darkness was already settling in. The six shadeless lamps cast odd shadows with their dull and lifeless light. Other than the cage, there were a few shelves, a couple of tables, some cabinets, and a whole lot of items crunched together. The door to a room directly across the shop area from the counter remained locked during business hours.

THE FRIGHTENING FLOYDS

Vicky kept something special back there. Something Papa Legba would rather her *keep* back there.

Vicky stood, came around the counter—passing behind Papa, who turned around and watched her—and then strode across the shop. Silently, she stopped at a cabinet, pulled a bottom drawer open, and began rummaging through it. Papa already knew what she was looking for and he was secretly hoping she had misplaced it.

No such luck. In a few seconds, she shut the drawer and made her way back to her chair, carrying the item. She sat looking at the little cassette, turning it over in her hands.

"I suppose that's *the* tape, eh child?"

"It is." Vicky didn't look up; she slid open a wooden door at the bottom of the counter and removed a vintage Sanyo Boombox 9965 and lifted it onto the counter. "Check this out. I've had this little retro horror since I was a child. My parents hated it."

"I imagine a lot more people are going to hate it by the time tonight is over."

Now she looked up at him. "They're not going to know about it."

"They'll see you."

"You're supposed to help me with that."

"I can only do so much, child. I can't make you invisible. I can only give you a deterrent. Someone might still see you."

"Maybe they will, or maybe I'll stay hidden enough. What does it matter? It's not like they'll live to tell the tale."

"What if somebody stops your pets?"

SLOTH ZOMBIES

Vicky scoffed. "No one can do that. Big Daddy Devil made sure of it. He said, 'No one on Earth will be able to stop them but you.' And you know, despite how deceitful he is, he never lies during a deal. He cares too much about his reputation."

Papa Legba removed his hat with a sigh, rubbed his head, and then put it back on. "Yeah, I know."

Papa Legba had given her the protection she needed: an aura of fear and disgust would surround here (as if that were anything new), encouraging people to look away. To further help hide her in the darkness, she would wrap the mist around her like a shroud. Vicky was also pretty slick when it came to hiding – so much so that her pet name for herself was Slick Vicky. At school, she would skip class and hide in bathroom stalls, behind dumpsters, and she even hid in the teacher's lounge once without getting caught; she once hid behind the bleachers so well in gym class that she was marked absent from class. This skill was acquired when she was young and had to hide from her crazy, abusive mother who chased her through the house to throw her on the floor like Piper Laurie and make her pray away her devilish inclinations. As one could plainly see, it did not work.

As she stood at the window, she marveled at the full brightness of the moon looming large in the clear black sky. Winter's constellations twinkled sporadically. These were both good

THE FRIGHTENING FLOYDS

signs: the tiny town of Pure Green was going to pay tonight.

Vicky went to the cage and opened it, reached in, and petted each young sloth. "You boys be good. Mommy will be home before you know it."

After closing the cage, she crossed the shop to the locked door, took the key from the front pocket of her long black skirt and stuck it in the lock. Before turning it, she said, "It's just me, boys. It's just Mama. Don't be alarmed." The knob twisted slowly as sweat formed on her brow. The creatures knew she was their mother, but one could never be sure about the actions or reactions of abominations. If their bodies were deformed, their minds could be, too.

A crunchy wood-on-wood sound preceded the opening of the door. Vicky covered her mouth and nose. Proper toilet etiquette *had* to be the next lesson she taught them. When she stepped in and peered around the darkened room, she caught sight of a silhouette rising from the far right corner near the bathroom; light shone from under the bathroom's closed door. Usually the creatures rested near one another, so she expected to see the others in seconds.

Expectations were met as she began to see several pairs of red dots form around the corner – counting them as they appeared: *two, three, four, and...*

One was missing – the tallest one.

"Okay, where is Five?"

Something then snatched her black sweatshirt at the hem; a sharp object barely scratched her skin as it slid easily through the fabric.

SLOTH ZOMBIES

That's why the smell was so strong.

Vicky turned to her left and looked up into the red glowing eyes of Five. Standing six-foot-eleven when fully upright, the mutant sloth—hunched over but still over six-foot—breathed heavy, meaty breath in her face.

Vicky grabbed its paw and said, "Let go of Mommy's shirt." The giant sloth did as told. With a motion to the others, she said, "Come my darlings. Come join Mommy by the door."

In the darkness of the backroom, with just a shade of light from the shop filtering beyond the threshold, the mutant sloths looked ominous: their massive silhouettes tall and broad; hunched and shaggy bodies with dangling arms and formidable claws backlit by the dim bathroom light; the slow, methodical gait of a dominant predator; heavy, dark-red glowing eyes that spoke of Satan's work staring straight ahead, rarely blinking. They moved through the backroom like dedicated actors in a haunted house, crouching, sneaking, limping, sliding their feet, ready to pounce at Vicky's command. Those claws could rip flesh to shreds; their teeth were fangs chiseled to a fine point by the hands of darkness. They may have moved slowly, but they were powerful and indestructible.

Once they gathered around her, she told them to stay and headed back to the counter where the boombox sat. Before hitting play, she had a few more words for them.

"Tonight, my creations, you will deliver vengeance to me. Vengeance for years of exile and torment, snickering and talking behind my back; for all of the spitballs and chewing gum in my hair; for all the times some meathead tripped me or tugged on my curls; for all of the hurtful names and evil rumors; and for all of the people who might not have participated but stood idly by while my life was ruined, you will teach this town that Voodoo Vicky has not forgotten and will take it no more. Tonight, Pure Green runs red—and becomes pure blood."

Then she turned on the tape and Dolores O'Riordan's soulful voice began to sing about the living dead that was in her head. To keep herself from having to maintain a continuous chant, Vicky exerted her mind control abilities through music, making the track her incantation. Since these mutated sloths were technically zombies, she thought this song was appropriate.

Oh Dolores – all the years you made a sad girl not hate herself has come to this. I wish you were here to enjoy it.

The sloths shuffled from the backroom's dark interior, ducking their heads as they passed through the doorway. Slowly, they returned to their crouched positions. Vicky took the basket of fruit and raw chicken and overturned it, tossing the food to the floor. The eager sloths swiped at the offerings and ripped them from the floor, tossing them between their teeth and tearing them to bits. They nibbled at the fruit, and even swallowed some of it whole, but they wanted the meat. If a sloth could get its claws on the raw chicken, they forsook the fruit. Vicky watched as they tore, chewed, gobbled, and swallowed the dinner.

It took no longer than four minutes for the abominations to clear the food from the floor;

SLOTH ZOMBIES

once the chicken had been devoured they returned their attention to the fruit. Now, their appetites where whetted and they wanted more.

"The time has come my children. It is time to gain revenge for Mommy."

Vicky then realized a moment too late that she had forgotten to open the shop door so the sloths could exit the building. But it was of no concern to the sloths, for Two, who was in the lead, placed its paws on the door and pushed. There was a cracking, splintering sound as the door broke from the frame and fell outward, half hanging off its hinges.

"Damnit!" Vicky said, coming quickly around the counter with the boombox in hand. Luckily, she had a very thick glass door that the front door had pushed open upon falling.

Thank goodness I left that one unlocked.

Vicky locked the glass door and left through the back. When she came around the corner of the house, the sloths were waiting, crouched in the shop's small parking lot.

"Let's go, boys."

Voodoo Vicky's was a half-mile from the main strip of Pure Green. In all, the town was only about three square miles consisting of a few working class neighborhoods circling a square. In that square there were a library, police station with a jail, firehouse, three diners, two grocers, four random knick-knack shops, electronics store, home furnishing/hardware store, school that taught K-12, courthouse, coffee shop, church, bookstore, post office, and traffic circle with a flagpole rising from a patch of grass in the center. If anyone wanted to visit Pure Green for longer than a day (which no one ever did), they had to stop about ten miles north beyond the grasslands and farms to find an inn; and if anyone wanted to dine at one of them fancy fast food chains, they had to travel three more miles to the east. Pure Green was in the middle of nowhere.

Where no one can hear you scream, Vicky thought as she followed the sloths, keeping to the shadows. Not that staying out of the light was difficult considering there weren't any streetlights lining the road into town. The lights ahead in the square revealed puffs of mist floating through the air. Vicky heard chattering, laughing, and hollering from the folks gathered in town. The sounds of car doors and revving engines rode the breeze. Soon, shrieks would replace those sounds as the beautiful symphony of suffering and revenge took over the night.

The sloth zombies marched to the Cranberries' tune, hunched and hungry, the flavor of meat remaining on their tongues. They would eat their way through Pure Green – tearing skin and tasting flesh. The song would play on, for it filled both sides of the tape, so all Vicky had to do was flip it when one side was finished.

They now drew nearer to town. Some had already spotted the mutants coming. They stood staring dumbly, like the hicks often did in Pure Green. In another minute, recognition had dawned and the people realized they were looking at some kind of dangerous beasts.

SLOTH ZOMBIES

Vicky was not afraid of people knowing she orchestrated and executed this violent uprising about to transpire. On the contrary, she *wanted* them to know; she wanted to be able to look into their dying eyes. Enduring their ridicule all her life had earned her that right. However, if she were found out too soon, and one of these brain-dead country morons figured out the music drove the sloths, she might end up on the bad end of a smoking gun, and if the tape stopped, the sloths stopped, and her vengeance would be foiled. No doubt someone would figure it out when she flipped the tape, but she hoped it might be too late before that happened.

She recognized two of the people watching the sloths come into town: a man in a flannel shirt wearing a John Deere baseball cap and a woman in a sleeveless pink tank top and blue jean shorts. The man was Billy Ellington – when they were in high school gym class together, Billy used to throw balls at her head – and the woman was Elle McDonald; Elle used to call her Virgin Vicky and constantly told her no guys would ever want her. Vicky never really gave a hoot whether or not any guys would ever want her, but she grew sick of looking at Elle's sneering, supercilious face.

Telepathically, she said, *One and Two – take out that man and woman.*

Their connection to Vicky's mind enabled them to know exactly to whom she was referring. One (the only sloth with a white and yellow streak down its back) and Two (had an off-kilter nose) broke from the pack and headed towards Elle and Billy.

THE FRIGHTENING FLOYDS

"Holy shit! What in tarnation are those?" Billy said.

"They look like giant sloths!"

Elle and Billy were too much in awe to know they should be afraid. One and Two were able to get within ten feet of them before Billy realized he and Elle were in danger. Two's claws were clicking and One was chomping its teeth together. The thirty-year-old redneck pulled out his Beretta and fired two shots into Two, barely causing the creature to jerk back. Billy emptied his gun into both sloths but they kept coming. The bullet holes closed up immediately. By the time Billy was squaring to fight, Two's claws were ripping right through his throat.

Elle screamed as she was splashed with blood about the face and neck. As she turned to run, she felt giant paws grab her on both sides of the head and yank her back. When the jagged, mutated fangs penetrated the top of her cranium, she shrieked. The blood squirted up and flowed down as the skull cracked. When One pulled its head back, the top part of Elle's head came with it.

While Elle and Billy died, Three, Four, and Five were passing Ben's Din Din Diner. Ben was a real asshole who spat chewing tobacco on the ground at Vicky's feet every time he got the chance; he often followed this up with some brilliant slur, such as "freak", "psycho", or "Devil worshipping bitch." Inside having dinner was Peter Monroe, the local pastor who loved to remind Vicky that she was going to burn in Hell for her sins, and it wasn't so much that he told her this, it was that he said it with glee, like the thought of her roasting in flames for eternity brought him delight.

Burn this, Peter. Three and Four, do your stuff.

Three (shortest of the group) kicked down the diner's wooden door. A large portion of it blasted into splinters, making the few patrons within jump. Peter turned in his booth to watch as Three entered and made a B-line for Ben, who was behind the counter counting cash on the other side of the restaurant. He simply stood and stared wide eyed as the creature ambled towards him.

Too intent on the scene inside, Peter didn't see Four (who had the longest, wildest fur) walk up to the window next to him until it was jamming its hand through the glass, sending shards of it into the pastor's face. Stricken with terror, Peter watched as Four pulled him through the broken window. The pointed tip of a large shard hooked into Peter's forehead and tore away the flesh as the sloth dragged him through. The man howled in pain as the shard slid over his left eyeball, ripping it loose and leaving it impaled on the glass.

Once Four had Peter through, it stood the man up and lifted him to face level. Cupping Peter's head in both hands, Four began to squeeze. Peter thrashed and screamed as he felt his cranium caving in. Blood oozed from his ears and down his forehead, and pooled in his right eye. The eye bulged in its socket, oozing out just a little. Four opened its mouth and squeezed as hard as he could. Peter's skull gave away with a series of crunches, shooting the eyeball from the socket and into Four's mouth. After the eyeball appetizer, Four licked the gooey brain matter from its hands.

THE FRIGHTENING FLOYDS

"Freeze!" someone yelled from the other side of the square.

Two Pure Green police officers aimed their guns at Five. From the shade beneath a tall Maple tree, Vicky had a good view of both cops. One of them she did not recognize, but one of them she did. Freddy Thomas – the boy who spat on her in front of the entire lunchroom and called her "spooky whore" in 8th grade, which was another nickname she carried through most of high school, and Freddy always made sure to remind people of that nickname when they were children; in fact, he still did it into adulthood. That stopped once he joined the force, but he still gave her looks of disdain whenever they passed one another and she could tell he was just dying to say it.

Hurt him, Five.

And the song played on.

Back in the diner, Three had already laid waste to Ben's employees when they tried to get in its way. They lay in crumpled heaps on the floor. Ben, who was large and strong in his own right, backed all the way to the corner of the bar and went under the counter for a baseball bat. He held it before him, waving it at Three.

"Come on, you ugly bastard." Ben swung the bat right at the creature's head and nailed it with a loud smack. The sloth's head barely moved, and it kept coming.

"What the hell?" Ben swung again, and the sloth caught the fat part of the bat in its right hand, and with one mighty pinch, the end of the bat splintered.

SLOTH ZOMBIES

Three tore the remainder of the bat from Ben's grasp and shoved Ben against the wall and held him there by the neck. It then jammed the jagged weapon through the man's stomach; the bat existed through his back and penetrated the wall, pinning him there.

Blood gushed from Ben's mouth as he looked down at the handle and knob sticking out of his guts. He tried to pull it out, but it was wedged too deeply into the wall, and he was now too weak to fashion a tight grip. But Three would help him out of his predicament.

With its mighty hands, the sloth pulled Ben forward by his shoulders. The knob slid through the hole in his abdomen and Ben popped off the bat with a sickening squish. Three then held Ben by his right arm and slammed his head into the marble countertop, splattering it like a busted watermelon.

All seven officers of the Pure Green Police Department had gathered in the square to take shots at Five. One, Two, and Four had joined beside him and were all absorbing bullets. The cops watched in horror as the bullet holes closed and the sloths kept coming.

The monsters' onslaught had been going about thirty minutes now, counting from the time they left the shop, and the tape still had a few minutes left. Vicky didn't want to take any chances, so she hit stop and quickly ejected the tape. The sloths stopped where they stood, frozen in the positions they had been in when the music ceased playing. It always took a couple of minutes for the hold of the

THE FRIGHTENING FLOYDS

spell to dissipate, and they would remain locked until it did so.

The cops were scratching their heads in wonder for a few seconds before realizing that this was their opportunity. They emptied what was left of their bullets, reloaded, and opened fire again. This time, even though the sloths were still unmoved, their wounds were not healing. The cops took headshots to try and drop them yet they still didn't fall.

From the shadows, Vicky saw her sloths taking these shots and quickly pumped the tape back into the player, hit play, and double-checked to ensure the volume was at its maximum. With Dolores' powerful vocals once again blaring through the night, the sloths continued their assault. All the damage the police officers had inflicted healed in a matter of seconds and the cops cried out in terror.

As the sloths drew nearer, the cops emptied their guns once again and, with no other alternatives left, they threw the weapons at the oncoming creatures – but the guns bounced off of them and skidded along the ground. The first sloth to make a move was Five. He grabbed two cops by their arms and ripped them right from their sockets. Both men fell to the ground screaming with their stumps gushing blood. The other five men turned to run, but ran into the other sloths who had somehow managed to maneuver around and come up behind them, thanks to Vicky's guidance.

Two had Freddy and another man, but Five pulled Freddy away because Vicky had specifically asked *it* to hurt Freddy. The other man found his head twisted off. Four lifted one officer above its head and slammed him down to be impaled on a nearby fire hydrant. Two stuck its left paw into another officer's stomach, reached all the way through, grabbed his spine, and yanked it out through the front. One bit such an enormous chunk out of the last officer's neck that his head flopped back like a Pez dispenser.

That left Freddy and Five. Through its eyes, Vicky relished Freddy's fear. *Do it now, Five.*

Five held Freddy's neck with its left paw, reared back its right, and jammed a claw into each of Freddy's eyes. Five then ripped off Freddy's face, taking the facial bones and all. Then, to finish it, the sloth forced its paw into the officer's chest and tore out his heart. After Freddy fell to the bloody street, Five turned around, spotted Vicky across the way standing beside a tree, smiled its sloth smile and took a bite out of the heart as if it were a pulpy apple.

Standing beneath the overhanging branches of a large maple tree, Vicky felt happiness for the first time in years. The warmth she felt for her children made her chest swell with emotion, and she found herself wiping tears from her eyes.

"Oh, you done a bad thing here," said a familiar voice from the shadows behind her.

Vicky turned and saw Papa Legba emerge from the shade. "A really bad thing."

Rolling her eyes, she said, "Did I?"

"Yes, dear." Papa stood next to her. "You asked the Devil for abominations to help you exact revenge. That's not a good thing, chere."

THE FRIGHTENING FLOYDS

"They deserve it."

"Who are you to say?"

"The product of their evil, that's who."

"Are you though? Are *you* the product of *their* evil? Or is that evil there in your heart?"

Vicky looked at the wise loa and knew he spoke true, but she didn't care. The need for vengeance had consumed her for years; she wasn't about to start feeling guilty.

"Guess you could say this is their sentence."

"By whose decree – yours? You are no judge, girl. There is only one of those."

"Then why doesn't He stop me if what I'm doing is wrong?"

"Do I really need to have the 'free will' conversation with you, Vicky?"

"Of course not. But I asked *Him* for help and got nothing."

"You got your shop on the outskirts of town, far away from your unwanted. Is that not a decent enough life?"

"I wanted revenge."

"Then what you sought was not noble. The Lord doesn't grant revenge requests. You were given what you needed and that's all anyone really has the right to ask for. Now, in your blind quest for vengeance, you have brought evil unto those who brought no evil unto you."

Damn you, Papa Legba, she thought as remorse settled in.

The old being smiled at her, removed his hat, and bowed. "I leave you then. I think you know what needs doing now."

SLOTH ZOMBIES

Papa Legba walked back to the shadow and disappeared.

Vicky prepared to recall her sloths, and just as she was about to, her concentration was broken by an unexpected call amid the chaos.

"Hey!" a man's voice screamed several yards from her, across the square from the sloths.

The call came from a muscular man dressed in a green shirt, khaki pants, and a red beret turned backwards; he was tall with large arms, and he held something in his left hand. The sloths turned towards him when he called. Many bikers and country boys in overalls and baseball caps, some in straw hats, were gathered behind the massive man.

"I got something for you, sloths!" said the man, holding up his left arm. "You see what you get when you mess with Pure Green?"

"We're gonna rain on you, sloths!" said a short man next to him.

Vicky realized the tape was not running – she must have accidentally hit stop – and quickly turned it back on. She couldn't call them back now or they'd be followed.

Finish it, she said to them.

The sloths began their march towards the crowd. The tall man tore the pin from his grenade and flung it across the square.

"Courtesy of Cpl. Bobby Higgins, bitch!" he yelled and those behind him laughed.

The grenade landed in front of the sloths and exploded. The people cheered as the creatures were engulfed in the fire. But the celebration was short lived as the four sloths stepped slowly through the flames while Dolores was screaming about zombies. Vicky had moved towards the square, in full view of everyone, holding the Sanyo high so the sloths could hear it clearly. The people looked at her.

"Holy shit! It's Voodoo Vicky! She's doing this!" cried Cpl. Bobby.

"I knew she was a freak," called another voice.

"I told ya that spooky whore worshipped Satan," declared a man in the crowd.

This was all Vicky needed to hear in order to justify her plight.

"Fuck it," she said to herself. "And fuck you!" she screamed at the people and gave them the finger. In doing so, she had to let go of the boombox handle and the left corner hit her in the head, causing the tape deck to pop open.

The square was silent and so the sloths stopped. Vicky put the tape back in and turned to the townsfolk before hitting play. "For years, you backwoods inbred, dumb-fuck hillbillies and rednecks have shit all over me...and I never did anything to you. You were all assholes to me, and now I'm going to be an asshole to you. I'm going to be the spooky, Devil-worshipping, witch-whore you've always asked for. Now fuck off and die!" The tape roared back to life. "Sloth zombies – kill them all!"

From the back of the crowd, Three began slicing men down. Bikers and hicks alike fell to its claws. The front half of the crowd, led by Cpl. Bobby, broke away and strode forward, leaving the rest to handle Three – of which they were doing a terrible job considering blood was spraying, limbs were flying, and people were dying left and right.

The mob heading for the sloths drew chains and knives. Some carried bats; some pulled guns. When the two sides collided, the humans swung their weapons, jabbed their knives into the hides of their enemies, and even fired their guns at point-blank range. All efforts were for naught as their weapons broke or had no effect, and the bullet wounds closed as they previously did. Soon, the sloths were tearing the humans apart. Guts and blood and shattered bones littered the street.

Cpl. Bobby met Five face-to-face. He swung his hardest punch at the creature's midsection and broke every bone in his hand upon impact. The uppercut he swung at the behemoth with his other hand yielded the same result. The corporal then fell to his knees. Five looked down at him before grabbing him around the neck and lifting him into the air. Five examined his face for a minute and Vicky caught a telepathic look into his eyes.

In high school, Bobby Higgins was the typical meathead jock who picked on weaker kids and wouldn't leave girls alone until they either agreed to have sex with him or reported him to the teachers – the latter of which never really helped. Though he never actually bothered Vicky, she found him revolting and symbolic of the very culture that cast her out as a child. So, watching this town hero die was going to be rather satisfying.

Though Vicky wanted to see his eyes when he died, she didn't get her wish. Five reached back and hit Bobby in the face so hard that his head

THE FRIGHTENING FLOYDS

separated from his body and went sailing through the air. The head went through the open window of a nearby pickup and hit some slumbering drunk right in the side of the face. The impact didn't wake him up, just knocked him over. Boy was he going to be in for a shock when he awoke.

Five examined the decapitated body of Bobby Higgins for a few seconds before tilting him forward and taking a bite out of the neck stump like he was an enormous candy bar. The others walked over and started taking bites as well. Soon, Bobby was that evening's dessert.

Vicky turned off the tape and walked into the middle of the square and stood in front of the flagpole. People were watching her in fear from all sides. Turning around, she saw the sloths had ceased their feast. She turned back to the people in front of her.

"Does anyone else want to try to stop my sloths?" No one answered. "You all cast me out – treated me like some kind of freak, all because I wasn't one with your backwards country ways. It's not my fault if your culture is football and TV dinners. I'm not responsible for your lack of interest in education. So don't treat me like I'm the villain who denied you life. You've done that for too long, and because of it, life *was* denied to people here tonight. I just want to be left alone – so leave me alone, or I'll bring my babies back and we'll make some house calls. Got it?" Still nobody answered. "Good."

Vicky pushed the play button and telepathically called the sloths back. Once she disappeared into

SLOTH ZOMBIES

the darkness, no one from Pure Green ever saw Vicky again…because they all moved away.

PUDDLE OF MUD: A TALE OF THE BAJAZID
by Kenneth Bykerk

The skull was an unexpected find.

Where some men take solace with rod and reel in hand, Paul Norkus found his squatting in a creek sifting fine sand in a shallow pan. Like rock hounds who search hillsides for semi-precious stones or wildcatters with tin cans in the desert, those who pan for gold claim their own precious few. Sitting beside a desert creek on a warm winter afternoon or a cool mountain stream on a summer day was all Paul wanted in life. Throw in some cold beer and a friend or two to shoot the bull with and Paul was happy. A contented bachelor, his weekends were free as were his vacations, time he spent pursuing his pleasure.

Over time, he came to know others who shared this pastime and friendships were formed. Paul and a small few began regularly corresponding by post, discussing the art of the hunt and sharing tips and resources. Before long, this small group of men would meet and plan a trip together. The camp would last for three weeks in all as some arrived late and some left early, but it became the template for subsequent outings which always produced good times, even if they didn't always pan out in gold. This little club, over years, expanded and then grew smaller. One departed with the sound of wedding bells, one passed away, and then another until it was just three bachelors, each stuck firmly in their ways, spending their middle years digging in the dirt together with their dogs at their side. It was the best of times.

These friends worked many hillsides together. All over the state of Arizona they traveled, finding hidden campsites along forgotten streams even hunters would never find. They toured the riverbeds of the state taking stock of where their luck was best. Some locations they found were good and some were bad. One creek they spent only two seasons at produced a fair amount of gold, enough to make it more than just a pastime. It was the most horrible place they ever tried camping though and after the second year, they'd had enough. There were as well some idyllic camping locations that were completely free of gold, ruining the reason for even being there. Then one year, when the three remaining were looking for a new creek to pan, they turned down an old forest road in the Bradshaw Mountains and struck it rich.

They camped that year in a place where the old sign marked the road in: Baird's Holler, an indistinct blur of miles distant. When they came upon a meadow surrounding a running creek, they declared their goal reached. The meadow ground was soft, the grass green and the creek that ran through it yielded more and larger flakes than any of them had ever seen. On the southern bank of the

PUDDLE OF MUD: A TALE OF THE BAJAZID

creek, the wider sward, were the remains of an old camp; bare concrete foundations stamped WPA and tumbles of stones that once formed half-walls for tents nestled amongst young growth at the tree line. They found it didn't take much digging to reach the settled depths in that creek and each pan produced. They all agreed this was the best they'd ever pulled from a stream and declared their intention to return. Discovery and research gave them the name of their creek, the Bajazid, and corrected them on where and what Baird's Holler was. It was an old, forgotten town further up, one just a couple of miles up the creek from where they camped.

Paul and Carl, both from small towns in the northwestern part of the state, had long gotten into the habit of pooling their ride. Paul usually drove but Carl had purchased a new '69 Chevy pickup with a camper shell off a lot the previous year. That was better suited for the roads they were taking than was Paul's old truck, and the camper provided a place for their two dogs to ride. Dave met them at a diner outside of Black Canyon City and from there, after one last properly cooked meal and a slice of pie, they set out for Crown King and areas beyond that. The trip in was long and tiresome; evening had fallen by the time they arrived at their meadow. The next day they traveled further up the canyon to the old town. Rather than looking around the few ruins that remained, crumbling shacks and earthworks not yet dissolved by rain and time, they went straight to the creek and to their great delight were even more surprised than last year. They were not even disappointed the following year when a bunch of dirty hippies had taken over the meadow. Instead, they set up camp downstream of Baird's Holler in the shadow of the old mine and happily panned the creek outside their tents.

For four years following Paul and Carl would meet Dave in his '66 Wagoneer for one last hot meal and slice of pie before heading up to their summertime escape, and each time they camped there on the creek below that old, forgotten town. The old mine, a scar collapsed deep into the mountain, was visible just upstream, but the old town was hidden behind a hillock that bent the creek. Their camp was set up on a flat stretch of land that sloped down over a small low, empty field of soft, fine dirt. The field was silt built-up decades deep behind a small dam of discarded stone, the result of a creek forcibly turned. It was perfect for the dogs and kept the camp out of sight of the road that bypassed the town. What lay further up that road they never cared to know. They had found their lucky strike, their ideal location to pursue what they loved best with just the amount of success needed to keep their shovels busy and their pans wet.

Paul and his friends usually concentrated their work just east and upstream of the old town. With their campsite hidden by the bend, they felt comfortable spending their days upstream in places not mined out or covered beneath tons of discarded stone. This year the creek was running low and Paul saw an opportunity to cut in sideways from where the creek ran through that silt plain beneath their camp. The ground was soft, yielding easy buckets of promising dirt to be sluiced and panned later while sitting in the shade with a beer. The results were encouraging so Paul continued there in that bank, searching for bedrock whose crevices he could exploit.

He was so engaged in his search that he came upon a stone at a foot-and-a-half depth as he cut in from the side. It balked at his initial attempts to dislodge it, so he slid the blade of his shovel hard directly into the soil above the stone. Very shortly, the scrape of the spade revealed a drop behind the rock and Paul exploited that, twisting the blade left and right as he shoved harder and harder down. With a resistance that felt like a rotten branch giving way, the shovel moved and the stone that was not a stone fell out at Paul's feet. His first response was to leap back for it revealed itself immediately: a human skull, female with long, caked hair still attached and features frozen in stalled decay.

When he'd assembled Carl and Dave, after walking the quarter mile needed to call up the creek, the three stood in speculative wonder at the find. How did it get there? Who was it? How long ago did she die? Was it murder and should they alert authorities? Had they come upon the work of some maniac? Chasing these lines of thought, they began digging back from where the head had come. There, a foot and a half beneath the surface, a body long decomposed lay in a simple dress which still clung to the corpse.

This cast a somber pall over the expedition even as the three convinced themselves that the body had been there a long time, much longer than they had been coming around, and that it had long been preserved in the packed silt. Still they had no idea how it came to be buried in a filled-in reservoir. What occupied Paul's thoughts was not her origins, but his actions. Whether she was from a graveyard washed out in the last century or whether she was a victim of violence, that didn't matter. The thought that wouldn't go away was the realization that with his shovel he had decapitated her.

As they stood above the body casting possibilities about, the rain began to fall. It started with large, spaced drops from a sky that did not look threatening. In the confines of that narrow canyon, their view in any direction other than west was closely held. They could not see the magnificent anvil-head spreading up from the southeast. Carl and Dave took the Wagoneer back up the creek to gather their supplies, their pans and tools while Paul staked an old tarp over the torso they had unearthed. They had slid the skull into a cloth sack and tied it to the rear bumper of the Chevy. By the time Carl and Dave returned, the rain was intermittent but never was it windy. The trees and the depth of the valley protected them from what gathered in the desert beyond the mountain.

Three spartan souls, independent men handy and creative, spent the afternoon under two canvas pavilions they had lashed together. With the flaps lowered to keep the wind at bay, it was a pleasant time shooting the bull while working down

PUDDLE OF MUD: A TALE OF THE BAJAZID

buckets of sand. The thought of a fire was out of the question with the rain coming down steady as it was, so they fixed cold sandwiches for an early dinner and drank beer to wash it down. Their dogs—Dave's three and the two each who traveled with Carl and Paul—all crowded the pavilion, not wanting to be distant from their owners with the increasing crashes of thunder coming closer. With that thunder came a darkening from the southeast, as the sun beamed out from its last refuge in the west. The sunset was spectacular: golden shafts playing over soft pastel yellows, sifting seamlessly to patches of deep blue seen through towering cloudscapes. As they paused in their work to admire this grandeur, they did not notice the swelling of the small field before them as the rain sank deep into that fine, thin dirt.

Within minutes, western clouds chased the sun to an early end while the anvil-head breasted the southern Bradshaws. Attentions were turned quickly to securing the camp as the full fury of the storm came at once. These men were prepared for such instances and collapsed their tables and weighted them down with what they could. Then they dropped the pavilions, draping the canvas panels over their gear and securing it with their buckets of sand. When it became clear the tents wouldn't hold against the wind, they collapsed them and hauled their bedding into the camper and the Jeep. Paul and Carl ended up in the cab of the Chevy, their dogs back in the camper. Dave sheltered in his vehicle with his three wet dogs and a carton of Pall Malls for company. This was all they could do, sit there and watch the storm from the safety of their cabs. This is how they would spend the night, wet and cramped. At least the lightning was amazing.

"What's that?"

"What?"

"Watch just out there when the lightning...there! See that?"

"See what?"

"The water."

"What about...oh, shit!"

The summer monsoons in Arizona can consume a day and drown a night. After hours of rain, the flat below them was gone. Instead a small lake spread out before them, the edge having risen to within twenty yards of their camp. To confirm this, Carl turned on his high-beam headlights. Sure enough, the water had risen dramatically. Turning off the lights, the two looked at each other and wondered if they were in danger of being overrun by the rising water. They had never had such a rain on previous trips. Fearing it might be time to take to higher ground, they decided to consult with Dave.

Dave met them in the rain, two of his dogs jumping out into the mud as well. Their conversation was rushed, hurried as the rain came down in gusty sheets. After a quick assessment of the situation, they decided to grab those items that might suffer damage, and leave the rest. A bucket of sand could weather a storm but losing their pans would not be good. Then they would move the vehicles up the slope just a bit, enough to withstand a few more feet of rising water. Why it hadn't spilled over the old, failed dam at this point they could not guess.

They were not subtle in their evacuations. As they had been discussing what to do, the growing lake had risen visibly in that time. Their excitement and energy was contagious to the dogs as well with all but one coming out to supervise the project. Pepper, a little poodle-something mix, would only poke his nose out the dog-door cut into the back of the camper.

The scene was chaotic: men dashing with careless armfuls and shoving them into the vehicles, while lightning flashed rapidly as if disparate thunder gods argued who had rights to that night. The sound was terrific, wave after wave of rolling noise tearing the air with strikes uncomfortably close; the dogs barked and yapped to match. The cacophony was such that the three men did not notice the change in the tenor of the barking until a burst of lightning momentarily turned the night into day. A headless woman in a torn and tattered dress was walking from the swollen pond, now but a few yards from the edges of their camp.

The next flash revealed she was not alone. The series of strikes that followed showed she wasn't even the nearest. Revenants, corpses dressed in rags ranged all around them. They were covered in a thick muddy paste battered by the rain to reveal the remains of mummified flesh. There in that freeze-frame lighting, Paul knew they were undone.

Paul did not know how he made it to the Chevy's cab. In the black and white strobe of the storm, he scrambled through clawing arms to the closest shelter, his most primitive mind acting of its own accord. He felt them tear at his flesh as the clawed hands sought to catch and hold him. He twisted and turned and then his hand was on the driver's side door. He pulled himself in and slammed the door hard. The crunch was audible. Shoving the door back quickly, the fiend whose arm had halted its closure was knocked back and he slammed the door shut again. Without a wasted motion, he pushed down the door lock and stretched across the seat to secure the other as well. It was only then he looked up and around at what was happening outside the truck. Like a drive-in picture show with a faulty projector, he watched the climactic scene play out before him.

Carl stood spinning in a circle, the shovel in his hands swinging in wide arcs. Unfazed to all damage done by the blade, the haunts pressed forward. As Carl's circle shrank and his shovel lost purchase, Paul saw his friend disappear beneath a pile of dirty, bare skulls. He watched in horror as the mob broke, leaving only one holding Carl tight, digging its clawed fingers deep into his shoulder and dragging him effortlessly toward the rising water.

Dave was at the door of his Wagoneer, half in and struggling, hidden behind the dead beings that pulled and tore at his legs. In bursts of violent light, Paul caught glimpses of the dogs. Duke, Dave's Great Dane, sought its master through the horde that pressed in while Pocket, his Corgi, climbed atop Dave from the back seat in order to provide defense. The other dogs were unseen, lost in the chaos of the night, their barks and howls, their shrieks of pain adding to the din.

Then, as the horror of intent came clear, as Paul saw Carl dragged into the mire of the risen lake, there was a sharp yelp. He turned just as Pocket flew towards him and crashed with twisted neck against the windshield. This was followed by a blast that didn't come from the sky. Through the torrential rain, Paul saw one of the corpses jerk backwards, half its head in ruin. Another blast from the Wagoneer and more bits of bone and mud and gore flew back. Another blast and another, and yet another and then no more. The macabre crowd that pressed Dave and choked his car door did not slow down or cease their pursuit, even when torn apart by shot.

Paul's brain clicked. He had to move, had to do something. With thoughts only of himself and his succor, he reached forth and turned the key Carl had left in the ignition. The Chevy leapt to life, the hearty roar of its engine a lifeline to Paul's stretched psyche. In with the clutch and back into reverse as one hand turned the knob and brought the headlights to bright. Panic took over at the sight before him. Carl was struggling still as his captor pulled him deeper into muddy waters. Dave was being dragged by his feet to the same fate. To his horror, Paul saw Duke as well being dragged. One revenant had gripped the massive dog's head in one hand and was dragging the animal against its will. The sounds of fear and pain the big dog made were beyond agony and its great strength was for naught as it was dragged awkwardly through the mud on its flank as if it were a child's stuffed doll.

A skeletal hand smacked against the window of the cab, then another and another as those fiends no longer engaged turned to Paul. All of them, all but those with burdens, moved forward in a closing ring around the pickup. He could hear but one other dog above the unnatural agony of Duke and that was Pepper, Paul's small black poodle mix. Sharp, fearful yaps coming from inside the camper behind him competed with the diminishing screams of his friends and the terrified cries of Duke. These were horrors, worse than any he could conceive, worse than the illustrations imagined by the writers of those pulp comics Carl loved so much. These were ghastly figures, all bone and wet, shriveled flesh. Their cadaverous faces glared at Paul in the cab with soulless malice. Unreasoned fear was the only response.

Releasing the clutch, Paul tried to back up but to no avail. The tires spun vainly in the soft, silky mud as panic pressed the accelerator harder. The truck did not move. The tires only spun. Then a cry of pain rose above the roar of the engine and the pickup jerked backwards as a large bundle of mud, blood and fur flew forward from under the front left tire. The truck went backwards but not under his control. It slid, the tires not finding purchase in the slick mire. Instead the truck started sliding, the steering completely ineffective. Rather than obeying, the truck slipped backwards down the bank and into the muck.

PUDDLE OF MUD: A TALE OF THE BAJAZID

Paul at first thought the four-wheel drive was not engaged. Then, realizing it was, he put it into low and turned hard on the wheel, hoping to gain control, hoping to get traction. The tires spun, the wheel turned but there was no forward momentum. Instead the dead had gathered all around it and were pushing, pushing against the useless engine and drive-train as the tires slipped more and more in the mire without purchase; the truck slid slowly backwards into the muck. The more he tried, the more he gunned the engine, the more futile his actions became. The soil beneath was without stone, without anything for tires to grab. They spun vainly through a century of soft silt gathered behind an accidental dam swollen with rain. The truck slid backwards as the undead horde gathered to lend their weight. Paul didn't take his foot from the accelerator.

Out the passenger window, Paul caught a glimpse of Dave in a flash of lightning. He was flailing vainly, unrestrained in that muddy water, the waves thick against his struggles. Between flashes, he disappeared. Paul saw no sign of Carl or Duke or any dog other than the one dead on the hood of the pickup.

He gunned the engine again but still nothing. The truck was sliding inexorably backwards, deeper and deeper into the mire and Paul had no escape. Outside his door a dead host waited, watched and kept pressed close all around. There was no way out without falling to those things.

Frantically, seeking anything to help, he pulled open the glove box and there was Carl's snub-nose .38. He'd seen the ineffectiveness of Carl's shovel and Dave's shotgun, still, the feel of that insignificant chunk of metal was heartening. Even if it was just a specter haunting his panicked thoughts, he did have one escape at least. Paul was determined not to die at the hands of these things.

He swung open the cylinder to see if the gun was loaded. All five chambers held unfired cartridges. One last thought of escape passed through his mind, one last hope of shooting his way out or at least trying...and then the ground dropped out from behind the truck. The jerk was sudden. The whole vehicle tilted back at an angle that left Paul staring up at the sky through a mud-streaked windshield and Pocket's broken body rolling back onto the glass. The sudden move also served to expel all five rounds from the open cylinder and Paul heard them tumble behind the seat as he scrambled to catch them. Loss and despair crashed down upon him, crushing even the panic of his most primitive mind.

The storm, as Arizona monsoons will do, ceased all at once; the rain ebbed to a light trickle. Looking up through his windshield, his mind blasted by the events of the night, Paul saw a tear in the clouds. Through that break, the moon, lustrous and full, shone through without promise. It painted the night with horrific clarity; the cadaverous nightmares grinning at him through mud-streaked glass and Dave, just his eyes and forehead above the surface, staring at him from lifeless orbs winking in the moonlight. He watched in that silvery splendor as the mud rose higher and higher up the windows. Soon there would be just the windshield and then that too would succumb to the mud.

How long he would last after that, buried in mud with diminishing air, fear would not let him calculate. He knew he could not escape that horde beyond, could not break that glass and flee without being drowned at the hands of those things. He did not want to die screaming. He did not want to die with rotten hands holding him down. He also did not want to die entombed, frozen under the muck. He did not want to die gasping alone without escape in such a sarcophagus.

Those were his options. Those were the fears that chased his rational thoughts as abominations of irrationality clawed at him through sinking glass. He sat there watching the distant lightning illuminate great caverns of clouds hidden within moonlit swells. He sat there listening in vain to Pepper's protestations as the space within the camper diminished with the rising waters. He sat there, his crotch warmed one last time as he contemplated whether it be best to die entombed in slow, quiet dread or torn asunder quickly in nightmare brutality. As he sat there, his mind torn between these two dooms, the nickel-plated .38 slipped from his numb fingers and dropped beneath and behind the bench seat. He made no move to retrieve it. He made no move at all. He had no moves left. He could only sit there and watch as the mud slowly crept over the windshield.

Soon there were no more sounds from the camper shell and no more moonlight played on the glass. All that remained was the faint glow of a stalled engine light and the slow rasp of shallow breaths.

PIRANTULAS!
by Angela Yuriko Smith

"Does anyone know what Dr. Brogan's Halloween surprise is?" asked Renee. "He sent me a message saying we have to come out to the Old Mill Bayou to see it."

The group she addressed was all biology geeks, a misfit collection of students from the local community college. They were as different from each other as the fields they specialized in, but their love of science, and Dr. Brogan, brought them together.

"Is this the message you got?" Megan held up her phone and hit play while biting into a cinnamon roll. The bearded face of their professor filled the screen.

"Happy Halloween! The perfect day to unveil my surprise." Onscreen he beamed, his face shining with excitement. The sun glinted off the bayou behind him.

"I have been working on a secret bio-chemical grafting experiment and it's worked! I combined all our favorite obsessions. I'll text you directions to where I am. Come in the morning to meet…pirantula. Bring your tents—we're going to camp and observe." They watched their teacher as he fumbled for the stop button on the tiny screen and then he paused.

PIRANTULAS!

"Oh, and trick or treat!" Grinning, Dr. Brogan hit stop and his image froze on the screen.

"Pirantulas sound *awesome*," said Eric. "Obviously some kind of new tarantula."

Eric was tall and lanky with dark bangs that hung over his eyes. He swept them out of his face as he sipped his coffee. He set his cup on a napkin covered in spider doodles.

"That *would* be your fantasy. As if 40,000 species in the world on every continent isn't enough. The last thing we need is another spider," said Renee.

"Except Antarctica," said Eric. "No arachnid has ever been discovered in Antarctica. Maybe it's a polar spider." Talk of spider territories continued until the group dropped their empty cups in the bus trays and split ways.

Dawn rose to find the trio tramping through the underbrush near the Old Mill Bayou. A private inlet, the area was hidden enough to be popular with poachers, partiers and Dr. Brogan. He was known to camp out there, studying the local fish and fauna and experimenting.

Though the area was never too populated, the group found it oddly quiet that morning. They searched for their teacher in silence, following the GPS coordinates he had sent. The humidity was already stifling, despite the early hour. Renee was the first to speak.

"What's all that up ahead?" She was pointing through a break in the trees. Visible between the foliage were the remains of a small tent in nylon blue and tan. No one answered as they moved forward.

"Is this Brogan's tent?" asked Eric. He took out his cell phone to check the directions again. He looked worried. Renee shrugged and swallowed nervously.

"I think so. Maybe this is part of his Halloween surprise."

"He would do something weird like this," Megan said softly.

The shredded nylon hung in the brush like markers on a trail. Through the undergrowth they could see more debris. Eric moved forward and the two women followed until they stepped into a sunny clearing.

There were the remains of a campsite in shambles, gear and shredded cloth scattered around the clearing. Another tent lay collapsed, poles sticking out of it like spindly bones. A bedroll lay slit open to expose dirty fiberfill. Megan covered her mouth.

"Dr. Brogan?" Eric called out. There was no answer. The entire clearing was silenced under the humid pressure of the sun. There was no buzzing of insects, no twitter of birds.

Renee picked up a stick and walked gingerly through the wreckage. She hooked the shredded tent remains and pulled it to one side, peeking in.

"He's not here," she said low, almost whispering. Eric and Megan had followed behind.

"If this is even his tent," said Eric.

Renee lifted the tent flap higher with the stick, and they all leaned forward to see. The stick suddenly snapped. The three of them screamed in unison and fell back in the loose sand. Eric elbowed Megan in the side by accident. She slapped reactively, catching him in the back of his head.

"Oh my God... that freaked me out," said Renee. She held her hand over her heart, feeling it bounce around, panicked in its cage of bone. They scrambled to regain their footing.

"It was just the stupid stick," said Megan. "We got freaked out over a stick breaking!" She started giggling, breathless and nervous. Renee dropped her back pack to the ground.

"This is just a Halloween prank. Classic Brogan." she said. "This is where the directions led, so this is where we should wait."

"Maybe he left clues for us, like a scavenger hunt," said Eric. He pulled a bag of chips from his pack and started breakfasting as he walked towards the shore.

"Hey! What the heck?" He tossed the bag of chips to one side and picked up another stick, prodding something on the ground.

"Hey—check it out! It's like some kind of huge spider," he said. "It's a tarantula!"

"What are you talking about?" asked Renee. She moved to look over Eric's shoulder.

"Holy crap!" she said.

Megan followed to see what they found.

"We may have just discovered a whole new indigenous species of arachnid," said Eric. "Look at that tibia." He poked his stick into the mess on the ground and held it up so they could all look at it.

The muddy mess of bristle, scale and jointed legs dangled precariously from the stick. Covered in mud and fishing line, it was difficult to distinguish features. The thing slipped from the stick and dropped to the ground, causing all three students to shriek for the second time that morning.

"Crap, I hope it isn't damaged!" said Eric. "Give me something to put it in." The two women looked around for anything of use.

Megan held out a clear plastic to-go box that had blown into some reeds. Eric took it from her and prodded the spidery remains into the container. He carried it back to the clearing where he set it down on a cooler. The three crowded around to look at what resembled large spider legs protruding from a toothy fish.

"Did the fish eat the spider?" asked Megan.

The other two were silent, their minds struggling to comprehend the anomaly in front of them.

"It's a pirantula." said Eric. His face was flushed. "Like Dr. Brogan said—it's a piranha tarantula!"

"I'm going to text Dr. Brogan and tell him we found his surprise," said Renee. She tapped a quick message on her phone.

A chime went off in the trees just a few feet from where they sat. In the shadowy thicket, a small screen lit up. Renee retrieved it.

"I think it's Brogan's cell phone," she said. She held it out to them, uncertain and silent.

"Maybe it's part of the surprise," said Megan. She and Eric looked at each other.

"Yea," he said. He looked around at the surrounding tangled tree and vine that pressed in on them. The bayou was too silent with none of the usual cacophony of frog and insect song echoing through the trees.

PIRANTULAS!

Renee scrolled through Dr. Brogan's phone and said, "Maybe we should head back."

"This is all just part of Brogan's surprise," said Megan. "A Halloween trick. Let's just set up and show Brogan that we aren't scared kids. We're scientists."

"Should we all sleep in the same tent, just in case?" Eric waggled his eyebrows at the women. Both gave him a sour look.

"I think we'll all be okay, pervert," said Megan.

"What?" Eric was grinning. "I just thought it might be safer. Excuse me for being chivalrous."

Renee moved to start setting up. "You're right. This is all just part of Brogan's spooky surprise." She peered into the plastic take-out container as she passed.

"You are the ugliest Halloween surprise I've ever seen," she said. "I think I'd rather just have candy."

When dark fell, silence muffled the camp like a sodden blanket. The only sound in the night was the bayou splashing against the shore. Exhausted from a day in the heat, the kids built a small fire to ward off the mosquito swarms and crawled in their tents shortly after sunset. Waiting for Dr. Brogan, the mood was quiet and tense. They each lay silent, lost in thought.

If the trio had been listening, they might have noticed the peculiar splashing—erratic bursts instead of the usual rhythmic wave-against-shore song—but they were not listening. The day had worn them out and they soon slept...until the screaming started.

The women started and sat straight up, wide eyes straining to see in the darkness as their minds shook off sleep. A high pitched scream filled the woods around them. Fight or flight impulses sent conflicting messages to their brains which, as a result, just froze.

"Is that Eric?" asked Renee. Megan just sat in the dark, confused, like a flightless owl. Her eyes shone in the dim light that filtered through the tent fabric.

"Who?" she whispered, adding to the owl effect. Renee pushed her way past and looked out of the tent.

The fire had died to a pile of embers casting a dull glow across the campsite. The coals washed everything in a red hue, making the scene look like a demented painting. Eric's tent had collapsed, and he was thrashing around in the folds of nylon and shrieking. Relieved, Renee giggled.

"Eric's tent caved in and he's freaking out," she said. She crawled out of the tent to help. In the dark, something scuttled across her hand. She yelped and scrambled to her feet.

"Ugh, something big just crawled on me. Toss me my shoes," Renee peered nervously into the shadows looking for movement. Something rat-sized scuttled past the coals, clicking.

"Eric, for God's sake shut up! I'll help you in a sec..."

Eric's arm found an opening and thrust out into the night air, with his head and shoulder following. His face shown red in the dying fire's glow, hair slicked against his head. He fell forward, still screaming, legs and waist entangled in the mess of tent. His other arm hung at an angle, dragging against the ground as he tried to scramble free. He looked to Renee, one eye

PIRANTULAS!

bulging in terror. The other eye was gone, wet blackness smeared across his face like ruddy paint.

From inside the tent folds something scrambled up over his shoulder, an impossible assortment of legs found footing on the writhing boy. A gaping maw of teeth shone in the firelight before sinking into his neck, already slick with blood. Eric screamed and rolled over, helplessly flailing.

"Pirantula!" Renee screamed before she turned and ran, barefoot, away from the camp.

Adrenaline flooded her blood and she flew through the night, whipped by terror. Blind, she tripped repeatedly in the underbrush, numb to the potato vines cutting her bare skin. A solo thought raced with her, driving her on: get distanced from what she had seen.

Back in camp, Eric's screaming had degraded to gasping sobs and then nothing but gnashing and grinding sounds filtered through the tent walls to Megan. She sat, still owl-like, with her bedroll pulled up against her chin. Against the dim glow of the fire, creatures were moving back and forth in front of the light, casting distorted shadows against the tent wall.

Megan watched the shapes—arachnid legs bearing finned bodies. They clicked as they moved, rows of razor teeth clattering together as they lurched forward, seeking prey. A skinny boy, Eric was soon picked clean and the abominations spread out, looking for a new meal. Tears ran down Megan's cheeks and she whimpered with fear.

Silence fell over the camp as the creatures paused to listen. One moved toward her tent, shadow looming larger on the thin fabric wall.

Megan trembled as she watched—a nightmare shadow play for an audience of one.

She looked around the tent for anything that could protect her and saw a lantern. She reached for it as quietly as she could but the bedding rustled as she leaned forward. The monstrosities outside the tent started gathering. Shaking, she bumped the lantern's switch and it clicked on. Light flooded her tent, casting her own shadow on the wall as an advertisement. The pirantulas rushed the tent in a wave, tearing through the fabric to the screaming young lady within. Megan was overtaken by the voracious monsters whose appetite had only been whetted by Eric, now a pile of stripped bones and ragged pajamas.

A mile away, Renee heard the screaming start again. By now she was exhausted. The adrenaline had evaporated and in its ebb the pain of her feet burned through her nervous system. She collapsed to her knees, heaving dry sobs.

"I'm not going to die... I'm not going to die..." She crawled forward in the dark to a pile of refuse. Broken televisions, slouching cardboard and other household junk sat, a dark testament to mankind's disrespect for his environment. Behind her, Renee heard something moving through the leaves and a clicking sound, tooth against tooth, as it moved.

"No!"

She scrambled forward, climbing up the pile of garbage in desperation. Around her, the rattle of teeth multiplied. Trash slipped beneath her feet and she felt sharp plastic gash into her leg. A television slipped under her weight and she rolled—a discarded trunk broke her fall. The chattering sound intensified around her.

PIRANTULAS!

"Please, please!" Her hands fumbled on the trunk's catches. They popped open and Renee rolled inside and pulled the lid down on herself, hoping that pirantulas couldn't pry the lid back open, that they would forget her, and that she would live. She could hear them running across the lid, scrambling up the sides as they searched for the meal they had followed. Finding nothing, they moved away as a wave, continuing their search for food.

Inside the trunk, Renee lay frozen, lips moving silently in prayer, until all was still again. The musty odor of the trunk wafted into her nostrils and made her sneeze. She tensed, listening for movement and heard none. Placing one hand on the trunk lid, she cracked it open. A few clicks in the darkness found their way to her straining ears. She moved her hand back from the lid, soundlessly, and hugged herself. Silently crying, Renee waited in the limbo of darkness.

After many hours, she noticed light peeking through the thin gaps in the trunk. She opened the lid a fraction to see the woods bathed in sunlight. All was quiet. Cautiously, she opened the lid and stood up, stretching her cramped muscles. No clicking sounds, no waves of monstrous abomination and no evidence of the nightmare she had just survived remained. The woods were silent and beautiful.

"Like it never happened," she whispered. Overhead, she noticed something white stuck in one of the trees. It looked like a large egg case, covered in gauzy filament. The size of a tennis ball, it hung there, gently swaying in the morning breeze.

Renee shook her head, denying what she saw, denying life to the fertile sac above her. Grabbing a stick, she attacked the gauzy case with vehemence, pulled it down and ripped it open. Hundreds of jewel-like globes spilled out, glittering and moist. She stamped them with her foot, grinding them.

"You will not make more of them," she said through clenched teeth. "No eggs! I won't let you." Sac destroyed, her eyes followed the web up to where it grew thick and tangled. Hundreds more of the egg cases dangled high above, heavy with potential, waiting to awaken.

Renee walked backwards, never taking her eyes off the dangling egg sacs. She caught the handle of the broken trunk that had saved her and started limping her way out of the woods, dragging it behind. Her only thought was to reach town before these creatures did, and hide somewhere safer than a broken trunk. And then pray.

THE MOUTH OF THE DEEP
by Stanley B. Webb

Arno Champion steered his tugboat, the *Festus*, out of the harbor. The pylons on the seawall blinked red and green. Waves attacked with hairy white fists. Storm rain pelted the wheelhouse's rotating clear-view windscreen. The clear-view's whirling glass disc abruptly stopped. Arno swore, thumped the screen's electric motor, then swore again. Rain obscured the windshield.

Arno stared at his reflection in the glass, the reflection of a man coarsened by salt and time, the reflection of a man who had worked hard to gain little. Arno's client stood beside him. The client's reflection looked young and soft.

"How old is this boat?" asked his client.

"She was built in nineteen thirty-nine."

"Just made of wood?"

"Mahogany."

The *Festus* pitched in the swells outside the yacht basin. The tugboat's old Nelseco diesel engine moaned.

His client grabbed a handhold. "What kind of name for a boat is *Festus?*"

THE MOUTH OF THE DEEP

"That was her name when I bought her. Bad luck to change it. What kind of a name for a man is Romeo?"

"Shakespearean. Are you sure that your boat can take this weather?"

"She can take it."

Dead ahead, a towering sloop emerged from the weather. The sailboat's gilt bows carried the name *Wolfewind*. Men in foul weather garb scampered around on her decks.

Arno spun his wheel to avoid a collision, and grabbed his radio's microphone. "Watch where you're going, asshole!"

"Watch yourself," was the reply. *"As a sailing vessel we have the right-of-way. And use proper radio etiquette!"*

The sloop passed inches abeam of the *Festus*. The crewmen paused in their work and showed Arno their middle fingers.

"That's why we're risking this weather," said Arno to Romeo.

Romeo turned to stare after the sloop, but the *Wolfewind* had vanished into the weather astern. "That's him?"

"Garrison Wolfe, the hi-tech banker."

"He's a banker?" Romeo frowned. "What does that mean?"

"Bankers deliberately lure boats into wrecks, for the salvage. The old-time bankers used to put running lights on a mule and lead the nag up the beach. A captain at sea would think that the gently rocking lights were a ship in a safe anchorage, then he'd try to come in but hit the sand banks. That's how Wolfe gets his salvage, but instead of mules and lights he hacks into a vessel's navigation system by wireless. He sank that gold shipment, and he's hunting for it just like we are."

"Then we'd best hurry. I represent the company that insured this shipment. The gold was raised from the wreck of the *SS Central America*, which sank in eighteen fifty-seven. We believe that recovering the shipment would cost far less than compensating the owners for its loss."

"Where's our destination?"

"I have a map . . . here."

Romeo's chart featured a large red X.

"That's the Mouth of the Deep!" said Arno.

"Isn't that in the Bahamas?"

"You're thinking of the Tongue of the Ocean. The Mouth is a local feature, a hole in the continental shelf. If your treasure went down there, it's gone! The Mouth is bottomless."

"Oh, dear."

Arno programmed the wreck's coordinates into his global positioning unit, then followed the device's directions.

The storm's featureless gloom darkened into evening.

"We have arrived."

Arno turned on his sonar and studied the three dimensional structure-scan while he tracked the *Festus* east and west across the Mouth of the Deep. A sinuous tracing appeared and disappeared in the scanner's screen.

Arno felt a prickle up his back. "There's something moving down there."

"A fish?"

THE MOUTH OF THE DEEP

Arno rejected his own trepidation. "Must be. A big school, by the size of it." A static tracing began to appear. "Wait a second." Arno brought the *Festus* around. "That looks like a boat, right on the edge of the Mouth. You may have gotten lucky. We can drop anchor on the shallows and let the wind swing us toward the wreck. Throw out the hook and we'll go down for a look-see."

Romeo glanced about. "What hook?"

"The anchor. Outside, in the bow. Up front."

Romeo pushed his way out into the weather. Arno watched the man approach the bow. Romeo staggered every time the deck tilted, stumbling to and fro between handholds. Romeo searched around the bow deck, then tugged weakly at the fluked anchor. Arno shook his head, and stepped out to do it himself. His sea-legs compensated for the *Festus'* motion. He lifted the anchor and dropped it overboard. Several yards of chain clattered down, followed by many fathoms of manila rope.

Arno shouted over the wind. "Snub that line on that cleat!"

Romeo tried to grab the moving line. "Ouch!"

Arno did the task himself. "You're the worst crew I've ever had!"

"I'm an insurance adjuster!"

"That's no excuse! Get your gear."

Romeo looked at him blankly.

"You brought your scuba gear?"

Romeo shook his head no.

Arno shook his head in exasperation. "I have some extra stuff you can use."

"I don't do scuba. I can't swim."

"Afraid of the water?"

"Yes!"

"At least give me a hand getting into my stuff!"

Arno led the way to the equipment room at the aft end of the trunk cabin and prepared for his solo dive. Romeo tried to help, but the insurance adjuster mostly bounced around the room while the boat rocked at anchor.

Romeo blurted "Wait a second!" and hurried out of the room. He returned with two glasses of bubbling liquid.

"What's this?"

"Champagne – a toast to our success!"

Arno took a sip, then made a face. "Terrible stuff!"

"Finish it, or it's bad luck."

Arno downed the champagne, then on impulse hurled the empty glass against the bulkhead. Romeo winced.

"Into the Deep!"

He stepped behind the windlass motor on the aft deck, opened the transom gate, turned his back to the sea, and dropped overboard. The ocean received him explosively, filled his ears and muffled the storm. Arno swam down, aiming his dive light toward the bottom. The beam reached into fathomless darkness. Arno hesitated with a chill in his spine. The ocean had never frightened him, no more than any sensible man feared her, but when Arno was young his father had told him crazy stories about the Mouth of the Deep. Never in his life had he dived on the bottomless hole, despite his common sense. He put his free hand on his knife.

THE MOUTH OF THE DEEP

Arno located the anchor line in the gloom, and followed the line to the rim of the Mouth. The anchor had lodged under a boulder at the edge of the abyss. He cast about for the wreck that his sonar had indicated, and found the sunken trawler on a ledge a short distance down in the Mouth.

Arno hesitated again. He thought that he saw something move in the abyssal darkness. Arno scowled at himself. He was not a little boy; he was a man with a job to do.

The name *Argo* decorated the trawler's stern. Arno swam across the cockpit to the open hatch, and aimed his light around inside the trunk cabin. The interior had fallen into disarray, but he saw little danger for entanglement. A wooden crate lay smashed against the forward bulkhead. Arno moved the box's broken lid aside and discovered a bushel of gold: antique coins, ingots, and raw nuggets. His pulse began to race. His fee was a small percentage of the total salvage value, but in this case that percentage might amount to millions. Arno reached out and fondled the precious metal.

Suddenly a tremor passed through the water. Afraid that the trawler had shifted toward the abyss, he launched himself out through the hatch, only to discover that the *Argo* remained secure in her deep grave.

Another displacement wave struck. Arno directed his light at the abyss, and saw a huge object. At first he thought it was a trunk of gnarled driftwood suspended in mid-water, but then the object moved, curled itself toward him, and he realized that it was a giant tentacle. Three segmented appendages, like skeletal fingers, groped from the tentacle's tip. The arm's sucker discs were not arranged along its underside as they were on a normal octopus or squid, but grew scattered at random all over the tentacle, and each sucker had a rim of dark teeth. The thing showed blood-red in his light.

A monster had risen from the Deep.

Arno pushed himself off from the *Argo*, and kicked up toward the *Festus*, expelling his breath while he rose to prevent a pneumothorax injury. The tentacle looped around and followed him. Arno drew his knife. The tentacle lunged at him, its fingers wide. Arno dodged away from its grasp.

Then, a second tentacle appeared from the depths of the abyss and reached up for him. Arno dodged again, but one of the tentacle's icy fingers curled around his right arm. Arno released his dive light, shifted his knife to his left hand, and chopped clumsily at the boneless appendage. The tentacle recoiled, bleeding dark fluid.

The dive light hung at the end of its tether. The beam speared into the abyss and revealed a multitude of rising tentacles.

He reached his boat, grabbed the *Festus'* transom, and breached himself onto the tug's aft deck. Romeo backpedaled from Arno's eruptive surfacing.

"Help me out of this stuff," Arno cried. "Fast!"

"What's going on?"

Arno ripped his fins off his feet while Romeo loosened his tanks. He dropped the tanks with a clang. "Pull up the anchor!"

Romeo dithered. "What's wrong?"

Arno swore at the man, and rushed into the equipment room for his shotgun. He loaded both barrels, came back on deck, and aimed out the transom's gate.

Romeo persisted. "What is it?"

A long heartbeat passed.

Arno climbed atop the trunk cabin, and scanned the sea around the *Festus*. He saw no sign of tentacles.

"Will you please tell me what's happening?"

Arno lowered his gun. "The old stories are true."

"I'm not from around here."

"The stories of the Deep Monster. It's down there, and it almost got me."

"Did you find the gold?"

The Deep Monster retreated from his mind's eye, replaced by the memory of the broken crate aboard the *Argo,* and the mountain of spilled gold.

"Billions," he said.

His head began to spin. Arno staggered across the cabin's roof, his hand reaching out for support that was not there. Romeo watched him intently. Arno saw that he was approaching the roof's edge, with a drop to the cold sea beyond, and threw himself down on the roof. He lay there while his surging brain calmed itself.

Romeo asked, "Are you still there?"

"Yeah." Arno sat up. He paused to ensure that his head remained still, then he stood. "What the hell was that?"

"Probably just the excitement. Do you feel well enough now to go back for the treasure?"

The Deep Monster appeared in his mind's eye, and in comparison the sunken gold seemed no more worthwhile than a pile of scrap iron. "I'm not going down there again."

"But, you have to, I hired you!"

"Hire someone else." Arno headed for his bunk. He felt unaccountably tired. "I'm getting too old for this."

"Think of the gold."

"I'm trying not to."

Arno took his shotgun in with him.

He heard the persistent knocking and the rattle of the cabin's knob, but Arno took a long time to float back up from his nap.

"Are you in there?" Romeo called through the door.

"Yes."

"Come on deck, you need to see this."

The sky was near dawn. The rain had lessened, but the still sea rolled. The breeze was a cold slap in the face, and so was the sight of the *Wolfewind*. She had anchored on the opposite side of the Mouth.

"When did she get here?" Arno growled.

"About half an hour ago."

Arno went dizzy. His vision contracted. He leaned on the *Festus'* gunwale. Romeo moved toward him sharply. Arno's spell passed, and he waved Romeo back.

"I'm all right."

"Garrison Wolfe has figured out the wreck's location. You have to secure the gold now!"

Arno did not feel well enough to work, but the sight of his rival's vessel hovering near his prize stimulated his ugliest instincts. He wanted the gold.

Arno swore. "I can't do anything with that monster down there."

"I've done some research, and I think that I have identified your 'monster'. It sounds like a specimen of *vampyroteuthis praegrandis*, the giant vampire squid. It's a deep ocean species, and apparently one of them resides in this hole. They only come up near the surface at night. The sun will be up by the time you get into the water, so you'll have no trouble from the monster."

Arno scowled at the *Wolfewind*. "How certain are you?"

"Absolutely."

Arno continued to glare at his opponent's ship. His ears rang and his head rolled, but he suppressed his physical discomfort. "All right, help me get things ready."

He slipped through the transom gate and into the sea. Besides his knife he carried a bang-stick, an anti-shark weapon armed with a shotgun shell. He also towed a large steel basket, which hung by a cable from the *Festus'* windlass. The job would require several lifts, and he felt anxious to finish before the *Wolfewind* interfered. He tethered the recovery basket to a cleat on the *Argo's* stern.

Then, a wave of vertigo struck him. His vision narrowed. Arno took hold of the basket and floated, helpless until the episode had passed.

At that moment, a shiver went through the sea. The monster was rising from the Deep. Arno felt too weak to escape to the surface, so he hid inside the trawler's cabin. He silently cursed Romeo for being wrong about the creature's habits.

A tentacle coiled up from the abyssal darkness, and loomed toward the sunken trawler. It encountered the winch cable, seized a hold with its finger tendrils, and yanked. The basket's tether pulled tight against the *Argo's* stern cleat. The trawler rocked in its grave. A second tentacle rose and grabbed the basket. Both arms pulled. The *Argo* began to roll toward the Deep.

Arno dared to hide no longer. He pulled himself out through the cockpit hatch, dropped his weights, and kicked toward the surface.

The tentacles let go of the recovery basket and came after him, their fingers ready to grab, their toothed suckers gaping and clenching like hungry mouths. Arno spun away from the nearest arm, and thrust his bang-stick into one of the suckers. There was a flash and a jolting report. The tentacle recoiled, trailing a cloud of dark blood. The second tentacle seized one of his flippers. Arno bent double and pried the fin off of his foot, then he continued awkwardly toward the *Festus*.

A third tentacle came up like a whip and slashed toward him. Arno turned his back. The tentacle slammed into his air tanks. He heard the sucker-teeth crunch against pressurized steel. The tentacle's fingered tip circled to enwrap him. Arno released his tanks, kicked himself out of the monster's grasp, and shot toward the surface, venting his last breath. His ears rang. His vision tunneled. He was not going to make it.

A tremendous pressure wave lifted him.

THE MOUTH OF THE DEEP

He struck his boat's keel, and scrambled up the *Festus'* curved chine to the surface.

"Romeo!" Arno's word sputtered. "Help!"

He dragged himself to the stern, then on board through the transom gate.

The sea around the *Festus* roiled.

"Romeo!"

His head jumped with vertigo, but adrenaline fueled him. The equipment room's light showed through the open hatch. Arno got to his feet and staggered inside.

Romeo waited there, wearing full scuba gear and pointing Arno's shotgun at its owner. "That's far enough."

Arno stopped, feeling befuddled. "What's going on?"

"I'm first mate on the *Wolfewind*. We lured the *Argo* onto the banks last year, but she sank in that hole and the monster wouldn't let us near it. The thing ate two of our crewmen." Romeo gestured to the waterproof satchel which hung on his dive belt. "We found a poison that's effective against mollusks and tried to kill the thing with dosed baits, but it will only take live prey. Garrison suggested that we give it you."

Arno's brain twitched. He staggered against the hatch frame.

Romeo grinned. "Saxitoxin is specific to mollusks, but it's none too healthy for humans, either. I dosed your champagne last night. The monster was supposed to get you then."

The *Festus* shuddered against a heavy impact. Wet, slithery noises crawled on board. The odor of deep slime tainted the fresh sea air. The tugboat listed hard.

Romeo said, "Step outside and shut the door."

Arno shook his head.

"I'll shoot you."

"You can't kill me; it wants me alive."

"I'll blow your knee out. You'll live long enough."

Arno rolled his eyes and dropped, as if he had passed out from a dizzy spell, then he spun himself across the deck and bowled Romeo over. Arno grabbed the shotgun, but Romeo had maintained a two-fisted grip on the weapon. Romeo got on top, and pressed the shotgun down across Arno's neck.

Suddenly Romeo screamed and jerked backwards, releasing the shotgun and clawing ineffectively at the deck. Arno back-crawled, coughing painfully through his bruised throat. He used the shotgun as a crutch to rise.

A crimson tentacle had Romeo by the leg. The man clung in desperation to the frame of the equipment room's hatch. The tentacle coiled its way up Romeo's thigh, and embraced his hips. The toothed sucker discs latched onto Romeo's wetsuit, stretching and ripping the neoprene sponge fabric, then they attacked his flesh, masticating and drooling noisome vomit. Romeo screeched. The man's eyes pleaded with Arno's.

Arno blasted Romeo's clinging hands with buckshot. The tentacle dragged Romeo across the aft deck toward the sea. Arno exited the equipment room and ran forward.

THE MOUTH OF THE DEEP

The water beside the *Festus* heaved, pillowing up from the Deep. A wrinkled, slimy mass, a living island the color of blood, rose from the Mouth and regarded the tugboat with a cyclopean eye. Dozens of tentacles lifted from the sea around it, flailing in the air like a lunatic's dream. The displacement wave struck the tugboat. Arno staggered against the wall of the wheelhouse. The collision triggered an attack of vertigo.

Arno followed the cabin's wall to the foredeck. His vision darted and leaped. He slashed the anchor line with his dive knife, then returned to the pilot house. Arno collided with the windshield. He followed the wall to the hatch and shut himself inside. Arno started the tugboat's engine and pushed the throttle to its stops. The *Festus* surged. He expected to die, and felt determined to take his enemies with him. Arno spun the helm and aimed his bow at the *Wolfewind*.

The *Festus* came to a sudden halt. Arno bruised his chest against the wheel. He looked through the aft windows and saw that the winch cable still stretched down into the Deep, where the recovery basket remained tethered to the wreck of the *Argo*. The windlass motor strained against its deck mountings. The planks flexed.

The Deep Monster swam up behind the *Festus*, propelled by unseen appendages. A big tentacle reached on board and seized the winch boom. The *Festus* shook. The planks buckled. The boom and windlass ripped free of their mountings.

The *Festus* roared onward across the Mouth of the Deep.

Arno clung to his wheel for support, too dizzy to stand on his own. The *Wolfewind* was a triple image in his eyes. He saw her crewmen running around on her deck, weighing her anchor and aiming rifles at him. Arno let himself drop to his knees. Bullets smashed in through his windshield above his head, followed by the sound of the shots. Foam appeared at the *Wolfewind's* stern. The sloop began to make way.

The *Festus* rammed her amidships, and stove in her ribs.

Arno climbed out through his broken windshield. Gunshots rang out. Arno flinched, but no bullets struck him. He climbed aboard the *Wolfewind* and ran across her deck. The *Wolfewind's* crewmen continued firing, backing away from their railing, aiming behind Arno. The deck tilted. He grabbed a line to stop himself from sliding back the way he had come.

A dozen tentacles crawled over the *Wolfewind's* rails.

Arno mounted the listing deck to the opposite rail. He grabbed a life-ring and let himself fall over the side. He positioned the ring under his arms and kicked backward away from the sloop.

The *Wolfewind's* list increased. The monster's tentacles enwrapped the lines and climbed the steel mast. The mast snapped and fell. Men and women screamed. The sloop's keel rose above the sea. Water rushed into the hull. The *Wolfewind* settled deeper into the ocean's arms.

It all looked like a dream to Arno, a nightmare of vertigo. He could swim no longer. He clung tightly to his life-ring, using all of the strength that

THE MOUTH OF THE DEEP

he had left to avoid surrendering himself to the Mouth of the Deep. His vision drew in tighter. Romeo's poison was beating him. Arno wondered if drowning might prove to be more merciful.

The *Wolfewind* slipped beneath the waves. Foam and debris roared to the surface in her final wake. A few crewmen also surfaced. Arno heard distant shouts, then screams, then silence.

Arno's symptoms began to ease. His vision widened. His head became steadier. Arno felt hope that the poison was not fatal for a man.

Then, the Deep Monster floated up from the depths. This was the fate that he had most feared as a child, a terror inspired by his father's horror stories. But, the monster did not move. Its crimson flesh had become pale, and its eye glassy. The monster was dead. It had eaten Romeo, and the poison that remained in Romeo's diving satchel.

Arno smiled at the dawn's golden light.

HUNTING THE GOAT MAN
by Pamela K. Kinney

Goat Man's nothing more than an urban legend the kids around here tell when the weather cools and Halloween is on everybody's mind. Since Virginia has the Bunnyman with his bridge, someone decided Maryland had to do 'em one better and make up a half-man, half-goat monster. A satyr caused by a scientific experiment gone wrong in one story; another story claims it's due to a deal made with the Devil.

Sure, and I'm gonna rot my brain playing video games, just like Mom says.

With Mom gone grocery shopping, I'd invited my friends, Ty Phuong and Lucy Bovid to play the latest game I'd bought: Monster Hunter World. This gave Ty an idea.

"Hey, I think it'd be cool to go monster hunting," said Ty, pausing the game after the creature had killed him again. "You know about the Goat Man, right?"

I glanced aside at Lucy to see her reaction and saw her deep in an issue from my comic collection. I turned back to Ty. "Uh, yeah, who hasn't heard of that lame urban legend?"

"Let's go see if we can find him," Ty said.

HUNTING THE GOAT MAN

"Because we're playing a monster hunters game, you think we should go hunt something that doesn't exist? Aw, come on, Ty." Irritated, I shut off the game.

He dug his phone out of his jeans pocket and brought up Google, searching for stories about Goat Man. "Goaty" (an affectionate nickname given to him by locals) had lots of hits. Ty clicked on the latest article written about the legend. "He's been seen again, three days ago, at some shack off Fletchertown Road. A man and his wife were hiking and stopped by the building to drink from their water bottles, when Goat Man attacked. Lucky for them, they got away."

I scratched at the side of my nose. "Real opportunistic. I would think the monster would have kept stalking these people until it captured and ate them, or whatever it does with its victims."

Ty clicked off the Google app and shoved the phone back in his pocket. "The legends claim Goat Man has been terrorizing the area for eighteen years. It says he escaped a lab after killing all the scientists and then attacked a couple parked nearby right afterward." He shook his head. "Honestly, Jake, always acting as if you know it all. Maybe you're too chicken to find out."

I snickered. "Yeah, that's right, dork, call me chicken. That's not going to make me do your cracked idea."

Ty stood. "Well, I'm heading to that area right now. I go ghost hunting with my friends all the time, but this takes it to the next level." He looked over at Lucy, who had put down the comic and sat staring at us. "Hey, Lucy, wanna join me for a little adventure? I got a digital camera, a night vision camcorder, and a thermal imaging camera that I keep in my car for the paranormal investigations. Maybe we'll prove to dipshits like Jake here that Goat Man exists."

Lucy got to her feet, stretched, and nodded. "Yeah, why not? Sounds like fun."

Fun? Did she actually think searching for something from a campfire tale was exciting?

Lucy and I became friends when she moved here three years ago. I never thought of us like a boyfriend/girlfriend, but I did take interest in the things she liked, in which was mostly video-gaming, schoolwork, and reading. But from the glint of excitement in her dark brown eyes, I could tell Ty's suggestion thrilled her.

I grinned. "Okay, if Lucy wants to do it, I guess I can try this monster hunting idea of yours, Ty."

Lucy smiled. "I'm glad, Jake. I've been reading about Goat Man in this book on Maryland monsters I checked out from the school library, and I had always wanted to see if he's real or not. It'd be fun doing it with you."

My heart went into double time. *Is Lucy interested in me?* Mom arrived home five minutes later, and I clamored downstairs to tell her that the three of us were going for a drive. Well, it's sorta true – the only way to get to the cabin in the article was by driving. She frowned as she put down the two bags of groceries, one of them loaded with steaks.

"Jake, I need you to stay in tonight—"

HUNTING THE GOAT MAN

"Why? You always want me staying indoors at night. I couldn't try out for football because they hold the games at night. Forget the school dances; you used the drugs and underage drinking reason. And we fought over me getting that job this summer." I paused, working to calm down as the heat of anger rose inside me. It burned in my chest like acid reflux. "Well, I'm going out with my friends and you're not stopping me."

I gripped my keys and barged out the front door. Ty already had seized his equipment and waited with Lucy outside.

Damn, Mom, what's up your butt with me being out at night? Because Dad left you when it was nighttime, leaving you pregnant with me? Or is it something else? I'm close to being a man, not a little kid, and you need to quit being such a bitch.

The burning sensation hit me in the chest again. I backed the truck out of the driveway and roared down the street. Both Ty and Lucy held on tight, not saying a word.

Clouds rolled across the sky, covering the moon and stars. My headlights were the only light tonight to banish the darkness. Not that they helped much beyond lighting up the asphalt road a few feet in front of us. The trees on each side of the road ghosted out and were only revealed when I drew close enough to hit them with the LED glow from my headlights.

Ty touched my shoulder. "We're here. See the gravel road? Take a left there."

I whipped left, and with my window down, I could hear the wheels riding the gravel road with a constant crack-and-snap sound. Goosebumps popped up along my flesh and I blamed it on the cold night air and not the sense of dread overriding me.

The truck's wheels kicked up gravel when I screeched to a stop, some of the rocks pebbling the dark shack. Before I could shut off the engine, Lucy flung open the passenger door and bounced out, followed by Ty, who eased out more slowly, carrying an armful of cameras.

I shook my head, thinking, *Such a geek.*

Pocketing the keys, I climbed out and banged the door shut behind me. I clicked on the flashlight I'd snatched from the glove compartment and stabbed the trees with its beam. I didn't see anything there, so I did the same to the shack.

I didn't hear anything, not even crickets or bullfrogs. The cabin's windows reminded me of dark eyes. A chill rushed up my spine. My stomach cramped, my heart hammered, and cold sweat glued my shirt to my skin. This building and the entire area spooked me. Neither of my friends was panicking; Ty had simply handed his thermal camera over to Lucy and showed her how to operate it.

Once Lucy had it figured out, Ty tried to open the locked door to the decaying cabin.

"What the hell are you doing, Ty?" I asked

He kept his eyes on the lock but continued using what looked like a hairpin to gain entry, twisting it this way and that. "Trying to jimmy this open so I can get inside to take some photos and video." He groaned, unable to get it to unlock.

Lucy called out, "Jake, Ty, look at this."

HUNTING THE GOAT MAN

We joined her and as I peered over her shoulder; I saw a big red image on the thermal's screen. I hoped it might be a deer, although it could be a cougar or a bear. Not that I wanted it to be a bear or large cat, but either would be better than the Goat Man. I didn't believe in the monster before, but in these silent woods at night, one might have a belief in monsters existing.

Ty's eyes widened. "It's big, whatever it is." He lifted his night vision camcorder and started filming, pointing it at the area of the trees a few feet away.

Lucy squealed, "Shit, oh shit. It's heading toward us." She turned to me but fumbled and lost the camera. Scrambling down to her knees to find it, she kept her eyes on the woods across from us. Suddenly, she jumped to her feet and screamed.

I wondered what the problem might be and though I was frightened even to look, I aimed my flashlight anyway.

Oh God, screw me!

He wouldn't, but whatever stood between the two trees in front of us might do something unpleasant.

A hulking shadow stepped out into the glow of my flashlight. It had furry skin colored mottled gray and black. Two large horns rose from its head to curve over like a billy goat's would. As it approached, I saw a face that was a nightmare mix of goat and human. A man's checkered shirt stretched over its chest while torn jean shorts molded its lower half, tight enough to be blatant in displaying the monster's maleness. It had a man's beefy hands and goat legs ending in hooves.

Exactly like a satyr, except satyrs only belonged in Greek myths and had no place in a forest off Fletchertown Road.

Goat Man roared and rushed Ty, and before my friend could escape, the monster snatched him by his neck. Ty was choking, held up by the creature as if he didn't weigh anything at all. A whiff of excrement drifted to me. God, Ty shat his pants. Hell, I didn't understand why I hadn't done that yet.

Goaty drew Ty closer to his wide-open mouth and bit his face. The sick sounds of cracking bones, sucking, and chewing filled the air. Terrified, I clutched my flashlight like a weapon, ready to fight if I couldn't make it to my truck.

A soft hand touched my back. "Wait. Don't do it. Don't kill your father, my father – our father."

I stopped and turned around. "What did you say?" I didn't flash my light on Lucy's face; I could see her despite the darkness. I couldn't understand how I was able to see her. I realized that she could also see me.

She looked grim. "Your mother kept what you truly are a secret from you, and that's not your fault. She should have told you the truth."

"What are you talking about?"

"Remember the story Ty told you about Goat Man killing those scientists and attacking the couple afterward? Our father didn't kill all the scientists, as lust overcame him, and he attacked the last one, my mother, leaving her unconscious and pregnant." She took a breath. "He encountered your mother with her boyfriend, killed and ate the guy, and raped her, too."

I opened my mouth to tell her she was crazy but snapped it shut because I knew she spoke the truth. Insane as it sounded, it felt oh, so true.

Lucy continued. "Mom bolted and ended up in Montana, where she gave birth to me." A shark's grin formed on her lips. "We lived there until my true self emerged one night three years ago and I killed her and feasted on her corpse. I discovered her diary and learned about the Goat Man, so I came here to investigate, and I met you – my brother."

I looked at her face and saw for the first time the same features my own held each time I stared in the bathroom mirror. She was my sister.

The eating sounds stopped and we turned to Goat Man, who stood over what remained of Ty. He pointed at us, and down at the carcass. My stomach gurgled like it always did whenever I felt hungry.

Why would I feel hun—

"Come, brother, I know you have been feeling the change, along with the hunger for human flesh."

I looked down at my feet and saw my tennis shoes had split apart and instead of bare feet, hooves ended at the end of legs that were covered in the same hair as the Goat Man's – my father.

With the hunger raging, I let my half-sister lead me to the remains our father had left for us. I thought I laughed, but I bleated instead.

CRYPTO CAGE MATCH
by William D. Carl

I knew it was a weird gig from the minute they contacted me, knocking on my door during *Wheel of Fortune*. Don't ask me who 'they' are; I haven't got a clue. But they have buckets of money, and even though I've spun at Burning Man and Ibiza, I'm still just a nightclub DJ at heart. Ten thousand dollars for a single night of turntable work was a third of what I pulled in last year. I signed their contract without question and was scuttled onto a helicopter pulling out of Portland International Airport, my crate of music at my feet.

They made me wear a blindfold while we were in the air. That should have been my first clue to the illicit nature of our business venture.

Besides the stoic pilot (who'd probably also been well-greased to maintain his silence), I sat across from the small man who had knocked at my door that afternoon with a contract in his hand and a hundred Ben Franklins in his wallet -an advance on the total amount. He'd told me names weren't necessary, but I could call him Ben. Cute. Still, his suit screamed disposable wealth, and his pile of cash spoke volumes to me. Rent was due, and it had been a rough year. Economic downturns impede attendance at the big parties, my friends.

Ben said, "You'll just need to perform for a couple of hours at the most."

"What kind of event are we talking about here?" I asked.

"That's none of your business. You play some music, and you get paid, and you never talk about this again."

"I'll need to know what kind of music to bring. Can't play Abba at a biker ball." Although, I had actually done so, once.

"Think cage match, big time wrestling," he replied thoughtfully. "Heavy metal, industrial, southern-fried rock, something to get the blood pumping."

"This isn't illegal, right?" I asked, not really caring while that stack of hundred dollar bills stared back at me from my chipped coffee table.

"You want the money? You meet me at the airport. You'll be back home before two in the morning."

So, there I sat, with a black cloth over my eyes and my ears full of the *whump-whump-whump* of the copter blades. I tried to make small talk with Ben a few times, but I was ignored. This left me alone with my thoughts, and my thoughts invariably turned to what kind of gig required all these freaky restrictions.

We landed suddenly, and I let out a breath of air when the machine touched down. Ben slapped my leg a few times and said, "We're here. You can remove your blindfold. I'll show you where you're performing."

CRYPTO CAGE MATCH

Yanking the cloth from my eyes, I blinked a few times. Even though the sun was setting beyond a primeval forest, I had to squint away the brightness. What I saw made me gasp in wonder. I stepped out of the helicopter, which was getting ready to take off again, onto a grassy meadow.

The clearing was huge; at least the size of a high school football field, it was surrounded by tall trees which stretched to the darkening sky. Being late summer, they were in full bloom, thick with leaves, obscuring anything beyond their towering wall of foliage. In a large square, four sets of cheap metal bleachers had been erected, one standing on each side. They looked like the kind you can find at the poorest inner-city schools near the basketball hoops. At the near end of the square, someone had erected a tall structure resembling a forest ranger outlook post. It rose at least fifty feet into the air, four thick legs ringing a ladder and topped with a box encircled by large, black speakers. I figured this would be where I was supposed to DJ the event.

In the middle of the four sets of bleachers, there was a giant cage shaped like a silo. Criss-crossed metal thatched the top in a graceful dome over a conical tower that measured twenty feet in circumference. Spikes held it sturdy, and long metal wires ran down the side into security loops in the ground. That cage wasn't going anywhere. One side had a door which was awkwardly welded onto the frame, and it was surrounded with multiple locks.

Ben hadn't lied to me. This was definitely some sort of cage match.

As he led me to the tower, I asked him about the nature of the match. He shrugged me off. We ascended the rough rope ladder that led through a hole in the tower's floor, and I discovered a pretty decent sound system up there. Four turntables, multiple CD players, a computer system to regulate it all – indubitably as high quality as the best nightclubs in Los Angeles. Once I was up in the booth, looking down on the cage and the arena, I saw speakers set up all around the clearing. This event – whatever it was – was going to get blown away by the music.

The sun was disappearing beneath the tree-line in a splash of red and orange that coated the unending forest in dapples of furnace-hot color. A breeze blew through the tower, bringing a chilling tease of autumn with it.

While I began to set up my station, Ben finally spoke. He crossed his arms over his expensive suit and regarded me with a cocked head and a bemused expression behind his old-fashioned spectacles.

"You're in for a real treat tonight," he said. "This is sure to be the big one."

I noticed another helicopter landing beyond the arena. Several men exited, along with one woman, and they headed for the bleachers in a cheerful manner. I noticed the diamond-beaded designer gown on the woman, the quality visible all the way up in my aerie. The helicopter took to the air again, and another made its way toward us. Ben noticed me observing them.

"The richest of the rich," he said. "One percent of the proverbial one percent. These are the billionaires that can afford anything, even a sporting event like this one."

A shiver went down my spine, and I asked the question I didn't want to ask. "Are people paying to watch men kill each other?"

Ben chuckled. "Don't think so small, my friend. Anyone in the *Fortune 500* can afford to watch two poor slobs beat each other to death. No, these fine affluent folks desire something more spectacular, something wild, something they'll never even be able to brag about at one of their hoity-toity dinner parties." There was a note of derision in his voice.

"Oh damn, this is illegal, isn't it?"

"Maybe. In any case, nobody will ever speak of it again. They'll just live with the knowledge that they were here. At this time. With a few hundred other billionaires paying five million apiece to watch the Crypto Cage Match."

"Uh, the what?"

"My company hunts down notorious cryptozoological creatures and pits them against each other, or, in this case, against a wrestling champion who's slightly beyond his use-by date."

"Wait, Crypto-what?"

"Creatures, my friend. Mythical beings. Monsters."

I laughed. "You have to be kidding me."

"Oh, no. You should have been at the match last year when the Chupacabra ripped the heck out of the Skunk Ape. It was insane, I tell you. Poor thing didn't have a chance, really. Not against those claws. I wanted a Jersey Devil, but I couldn't find one in time, so the Skunk Ape was the best I could locate."

"You hunt down monsters and battle them against one another for a bunch of big spenders to get their jollies?" I asked, incredulous. "Wouldn't you make more money showing them live to the public? Let alone the whole question of the morality of it all . . ."

"Shut the door right there on the morality issues. I'll walk away from tonight with a couple hundred million dollars. That's free and clear. Don't even have to pay taxes on it."

Another helicopter landed, disgorging a handful of giggling women in fur coats. I saw a tiara in one lady's hair.

"I'll be as good as any of them. Bastards. I'll do this a few more times, and then they'll see me. Then, they'll see me. I might even be better than any of them," he said softly. He pulled a bottle of champagne from a mini-fridge and popped the cork. It spilled on his calf-skin shoes.

"So, who's fighting tonight?" I asked, genuinely curious despite my revulsion at the idea of an unclassified species duking it out to the death. "What's on the menu?"

"The most elusive of all cryptozoological creatures. A native of this area. I hunted it for years, nearly a decade until I found one."

He leaned forward, handing me a glass of champagne. He clinked his glass against mine and said, "Bigfoot."

"Come on, that's just a legend. Nobody actually believes such a thing exists."

CRYPTO CAGE MATCH

"Oh, it exists, all right. In my hunts, I found evidence supporting the fact that several communities of the beasts inhabit these woods. They're sneaky bastards, however, so it took me a long time to acquire one. But I did. And he's fighting tonight, whether he likes it or not."

"And I am playing the musical accompaniment to its death."

"Or the death of Rowdy Mike, its opponent."

I remembered Rowdy Mike, a pro-wrestler who'd done really well for over a decade. He was incredibly muscular, probably working out with weights in his sleep, but he'd had a penchant for dog-fighting, which had led to his fall from fan favor. I remember the pictures of him and his kennels of pit bulls, mauled and tortured. Yeah, I'd be rooting for the Bigfoot.

The well-heeled spectators kept arriving until the bleachers were full and several disgruntled aristocrats had to remain standing. They were making a party of the event, toasting each other with glasses of imported champagne and uniformed venders wandered the stands, hawking caviar and foie gras. I finished my preparations, opting to start the show with Guns N' Roses. "Welcome to the Jungle" never seemed so appropriate.

"You can start the music anytime," Ben said. "But, when I make the opening announcements from the inside before we bring in the fighters, I want silence. When I give you the signal, you can start playing again. Do I need to remind you that you signed a contract with a gag order? You can't speak about this night ever. Not to the police. Not to PETA. Not even to your family."

"Why me?" I asked as Ben was leaving. "Didn't you ever have music before?"

"I sure did. But the last DJ was killed when he got too close to the Mothman's pen. Tore his head clean off his shoulders."

I gulped, still not quite believing everything I was hearing. This was insane. However, I was being paid very well for a few hours of work, so I started the first song, the woods echoing with the strains of Slash's classic guitar riff. The crowd clapped and whooped their approval.

And I was off, changing records without thinking about it, moving from one turntable to the next, creating an aural wall of sound that erupted until I saw Ben stepping into the cage. He gave me a little nod, and I potted down the music.

Turns out, Ben is quite the showman. He announced the match; he spoke a bit about Rowdy Mike's history and notoriety before the muscular man, wearing a fringe jacket and leather pants, entered the ring to tepid applause. He raised his hands over his head and whipped the jacket from his shoulders, exposing his shaved bare chest. Then, he strutted around the ring a few times, posing long after the semi-appreciative clapping ceased.

In hushed tones, Ben launched into the mythology of Bigfoot, ignoring the half-naked man behind him. He related how he'd hunted the creature, explained all the scientific gobbledygook about the various equipment utilized, and the eventual capture of the savage beast.

CRYPTO CAGE MATCH

At this point he paused, escalating the suspense. Now, I admit that up until then I had been expecting some tall guy in a ridiculous costume from a 1970s drive-in movie to make an appearance. With Ben's extended silence, the tension in the arena grew to a firebrand point. The only sounds were the insects buzzing and the slight hissing of the speakers. Everyone, myself included, leaned forward, forgetting everything except the anticipation of Ben's next words.

"Ladies and gentlemen," he finally announced the familiar words louder than expected. "Without further ado, I give you the terror of the Pacific Northwest. . . Sasquatch!"

From a clever hiding place behind the trees, a metal cage on wheels was carted out. The bars were welded closely together, obscuring a clear view of whatever moved within it. Six strong men pushed and pulled at the cage, and a shadow shifted inside, leaning one way and then the other. Whatever it was, it was huge – too large to be a man in a suit unless he was some kind of freak.

Ben stepped out of the giant silo-cage as the six guys shoved the smaller one tight against the doorway. They switched a few locks, securing the two enclosures together. I stole a look at Rowdy Mike, and the poor bastard looked like he was going to lose it any second. He was sweating more than usual, and, even from where I watched, he looked as if he was shrinking into himself, growing smaller by the minute. He took a step backward.

Ben raised the microphone to his lips, watching the agitated shape inside the smaller cage. "Let the sixth Crypto Cage Match. . . begin!" He flourished his arms into the air and gave me a nod.

The crowd rose to its feet, cheering and clapping their hands as I started turntable three and a familiar techno beat surged from the speakers. Two of the six men pulled a lever, and a door snapped open between the two cages

The crowd screamed, stomped their feet.

Ben took a few steps to the side and peered through the bars.

Rowdy Mike looked like he wanted out of the whole deal.

I leaned forward.

And an eight-foot-tall beast stepped into the giant cage. It was covered in dark fur, speckled with lighter hair in thinner patches. Its eyes glowed yellow, and its ears were elongated like a canine's. A thin, pink scar ran across its face like lightning imprinted into the fur. Its arms extended nearly to the ground, ending in huge hands that clenched into cannonballs. Even so, I could see the black talons that tipped its fingers, sharp and dark as obsidian. It took a step forward, its feet as oversized as its fists. Its toes curled in a simian manner, and each ended in a wicked black claw. It took another step, turned its head back and forth as if sizing up its new environment.

When its jaundiced gaze locked on Rowdy Mike, it released a howl that drowned out my booming music. It started low, and then it rose in volume as well as pitch. Chills broke out on my skin as I heard that war cry. It was ominous, terrifying, and pitiable at the same time. It enveloped everyone, and most of the audience resumed their seats. The sound encompassed the emptiness of the forest, a primeval yearning for a primeval world.

And a raging hatred for whatever species invaded its territory.

I changed the song, finding something very Molly Hatchet about the whole scenario. The country rock, edged on with a mix of throbbing drumbeats, filled the big outdoors as if it belonged there. I smiled with satisfaction.

That's when Bigfoot (it was hard to think of the creature by any other name with those gigantic stompers) made a dash at Rowdy Mike. The wrestler ducked to the side a second later, and the monster smashed into the bars. Mike swept his foot at the beast's legs, trying to trip it, but Bigfoot only howled and spun on the man.

When they were that close together, it was terrifying to compare the enormity of the beast to the size of Rowdy Mike as it towered over him. It had to be two feet taller, and the muscles shifting under its coarse fur were muscles that were used consistently every day of its life. These weren't body-builder muscles born in a gymnasium. These muscles were earned by the hardest labor, such as pulling down trees, lifting massive logs, and rolling heavy boulders.

The monster made a grab for Mike, but it missed and the wrestler dropped to the ground, scuttling backwards out of the Bigfoot's reach. It stretched out those protracted arms, swiping at air. Mike leapt to his feet in a show of bravado that had the crowd roaring. He hopped onto the monster's back and started pummeling its sides, probably assuming that's where the kidneys were located. The thing gave a loud moan, flipped over, and dropped onto its back, squashing Mike into the dirt. Rolling to its feet, it revealed the wrestler, who clutched at his deltoid under his arm, covering a ragged, bleeding wound.

I switched the music to a little Foghat and threw in some Run DMC over top of it. I had to concentrate even harder than usual, since I really just wanted to watch this insane spectacle taking place beneath me.

The beast grabbed the wrestler by one of his ankles and jerked him upwards. Rowdy Mike clawed at the ground, trying to break the creature's grip. Holding the man in the air, the Sasquatch whipped its arm, shaking the human like a rag doll. The crowd jumped to its feet, cheering as the monster lifted Rowdy Mike and dropped him into a heap. . The beast swung him around in a circle by his ankle. Mike shook himself, trying to escape the thing's clutches, but it had a tight grasp on him. This time when the monster swung him, Mike's head smacked the metal cage. There was a snapping, crunching sound I could hear all the way up in my tower. The top of Rowdy Mike's skull collapsed in upon itself as it smacked into one bar, then the next one took it clean off. Blood and brains exploded.

When the beast dropped Mike, the wrestler collapsed into a twisted pile of broken bone. He didn't move, and I knew he was dead. The crowd moaned, disappointed at the short duration of the fight.

CRYPTO CAGE MATCH

Then, the creature made certain of its opponent's demise. It tore the arms and legs from the man like a wicked child with an insect. Then, it stood triumphantly over the bloody corpse, and it howled, that same mournful howl it had released before the match.

My record finished as the beast was wailing. The arena was suddenly enveloped in stunned silence; I myself stood frozen with shock, watching this death scene, unable to look away from the gruesome sight. The needle on the turntable reached the end of the record, emitting a *shush-shush-shush* sound through the speakers. Numb, I switched it off. Even the blood-sport fans in their bleachers remained quiet, astonished by the violence.

The creature howled again that eerie, doleful sound. It reminded me of whale songs I had heard – long, starting low on a musical scale and climbing in a long, graceful arc of loneliness.

Then, from the dense surrounding woods, came an answering cry. This one started even lower, deeper in tone, but rising just as high. It echoed through the trees, making it difficult to pinpoint its initial direction.

The creature in the cage lifted its face to the dark sky and cried out again.

This time, there were three different howling replies from several different directions. Once again, I couldn't discern where they originated from.

The audience in the bleachers was growing restless with the knowledge that there was more than one Sasquatch in the vicinity. The sounds kept coming, woeful cries and howls like those of the great apes in Africa. It sounded as if there were dozens of them.

And the sounds were getting closer to the arena.

In the distance, I heard the resonance of an approaching helicopter, the first flight back to the city. It was nearly drowned out by the primitive sounds of the beasts baying to each other, communicating in some crude manner.

Ben stood next to the cage again, a microphone in his hand. "Your transport is on its way, ladies and gentleman," he said, and I caught a quiver in his voice. "Please walk calmly to the landing area. No pushing or shoving. Wasn't that an amazing battle, folks?"

Nobody answered, but the people were all scrambling over each other to distance themselves from the bleachers. Many of the women tripped in their long gowns and high heels.

And suddenly, the Sasquatches were everywhere.

They came out of the night like hulking specters, scuttling out of the forest, separating themselves from the sticky darkness of the woods. The audience screamed and scattered, seeking cover. One of the beasts raised a generator over its head and tossed it into the woods. With a loud pop, the electricity blew out. I noticed Ben grab hold of the rope ladder to my tower, hauling himself up with an agility I hadn't suspected he possessed. He stepped into the room, pulled the ladder up behind himself, and slammed the trap

CRYPTO CAGE MATCH

door shut. Spinning to face me, he asked, "What?"

Beneath us, the wealthy people were screaming in pain as the two dozen or so Sasquatch tore into their tender flesh. I heard bones snapping, a wet noise as meat was rent, and short, gurgling sounds. One by one, the screams ceased as the richest people in America were ripped limb from limb, their designer suits and gowns stained crimson.

I whispered at Ben, "Those people down there . . ."

". . . are dead," he finished my sentence for me. "There's nothing we can do now except wait it out up here. The helicopters will arrive soon. I heard one coming a minute ago."

Somewhere beneath us, a man was calling for help, his cries distorted by the blood in his throat. There was a wrenching noise, and a loud grunt as one of the monsters ended his agony. It howled in triumph.

I peeked over the edge of the tower's window, the cage in the center of the meadow filling my view. Several of the creatures were shuffling around the metal, sniffing it, touching it. The beast caught within the cage stood near the door, grunting its impatience. It made motions at the area where its smaller cage had been locked onto the larger silo. In a few moments, the beasts had puzzled out the locks, switching them until they could shove the transport cage out of the doorway. Once it was able, the original Bigfoot stepped into the meadow, greeting its saviors. In another moment, it was scanning the horizon. It looked up at the tower, and I saw its lightning-like scar gleaming in the moonlight. Its golden eyes narrowed before it made for the woods.

One by one, the creatures howled mournfully and huffed at each other, short bursts of breath that reminded me of impatient dogs. Eventually, they all disappeared into the trees from whence they'd emerged. The shadows of gathering clouds blocked the light of the moon. The electricity hadn't ever switched back on, and the darkness permeated the clearing.

The sound of an approaching helicopter reached us, and Ben peered out upon the horizon, completely ignoring the evidence of the massacre beneath him.

"They're coming," he said. "Right on time. Let's get out of here, my friend."

I bristled a little at the 'my friend' bit.

In moments, he had opened the trap door and released the ladder, which hit the ground with a soft thud. He was halfway down when the whirlybird descended to the home-made air strip on the opposite side of the cage. Ben dropped to the earth and ran for the hovering machine, waving his hands over his head and shouting something unintelligible.

Call me overly cautious, but I didn't immediately take to the getaway route. Something about the way the scarred Sasquatch had glared at the tower had stuck with me. I leaned out, looking across the top of the empty cage with its ruined door.

Just as the helicopter was about to set down, a lone Bigfoot ran from the cover of the forest and grasped the machine in its gigantic hands. It lifted, tilting the helicopter to a 45-degree angle, and the blades slammed into the ground. Metal screeched and a blade tore loose, cart-wheeling through the air as the next blade snapped off the rotor. The whirly-bird was ruined, little more than a pile of junk. The pilot had fallen to the side and was pawing at the Plexiglas dome.

Halfway across the field, Ben stopped as the Sasquatch destroyed his escape vehicle. From all surrounding sides, its companions emerged from the woods, silently stalking and encircling the man who had captured and tortured one of their own. I counted twenty-five before I slowly moved to the trapdoor of the watchtower and quietly pulled the ladder back up into my little room. Then, I peeked over the edge to watch as the colony of Sasquatch headed toward Ben, their eyes glowing yellow in the moonlight.

"No! Don't!" Ben screamed, the sound bouncing from tree to tree.

One of the creatures started howling. Then, another joined it, then another, and another. Their mouths stretched too wide with the cries, exposing ragged yellow teeth, twice as large as a human's. The sound became deafening, and Ben dropped to his knees, his hands covering his ears in a futile attempt to block the terrible bellow.

The scarred Sasquatch lumbered over to the circle of his brethren and pushed two of them aside. They closed the ring behind him, and the huge monster stopped in front of Ben. It waited for the promoter to look at it, to acknowledge it. Ben stared at the ground, and I think he was crying.

The creatures all fell silent, ceasing their howls and grunts. The meadow was eerily still, with the band of Sasquatch standing around Ben and his one-time captive. The silence extended until the scarred beast gently placed a hand beneath Ben's chin and lifted the man's face so it could stare into the human's eyes. For at least a minute, Ben was forced to peer into the yellow gaze of the monster, to look upon the face of something he had enslaved.

"Please. . . "He whispered. The meadow was so quiet I could hear his hushed plea as if he stood merely a few feet away from me.

The scar-faced beast tilted its head, as if seeking answers from this puny, pathetic human. Then, with a single wrench, it separated Ben's head from his body. I looked away, stifling a cry of horror. I put my fist in my mouth so I wouldn't scream, and I stayed that way for several excruciating minutes. Finally, I looked over the ledge at the arena. The meadow was littered with corpses, including Ben's, but the Sasquatch had disappeared into the woods as silently as they'd come.

I waited until the next helicopter landed and the pilot emerged, calling for any passengers. He cursed when he saw the carnage, and he was getting ready to take off for the city when I ran out to him. I hurried as fast as I could, praying none of the monsters would leap from a hiding place and tear me to shreds. Miraculously, I got to the copter without seeing any of the things, and I was back in the city in a half hour. The pilot took off for places unknown, and I went back to my shabby apartment.

I haven't spoken to anyone about the cage match. I doubt anyone would believe me. There was never a news report about the discovery of a huge cage in the middle of the forest and a few hundred dead rich people. I know; I looked for it. Ben had mentioned his influence, and it appeared to be just as effective from the grave.

I somehow emerged unscathed from the tragedy. At least, physically. At night, whenever I close my eyes to try to sleep, I hear that terrible howling in the woods, starting low and rising in tone and volume. It's the sound of something dark and fetid and bestial.

It plays over and over like a record in my skull.

And I wait for the inevitable day when the record gives way to the *shush-shush-shush* at the end.

THE TRIALS OF DR. RAINS
by Matthew M. Montelione

Shoreham, Eastern Long Island, New York. August 1916.

Helen Rains awoke to the soft chirping of birds outside her window. With a yawn, she rose and drew the curtains. Sunlight streamed in, the warm rays readying her for the new day. *There's nothing like a hot summer's day*, she thought as she got dressed. Her mother was still asleep, and her father was, not surprisingly, already working in his greenhouse. After a quick breakfast, she went outside, excited to tend to the garden.

Helen smiled as she patted down loose soil around the bell pepper plants. Though she sweated profusely, she loved the humid and sea-soaked Long Island air. Summertime rendered her altogether happy and energetic. However, after spending many hours gardening, it was time to head inside. Her father, Dr. Walter Rains, warned her last night that a thunderstorm was expected in the late afternoon, and thick gray clouds already encroached on the sun.

Helen stood up, brushing the dirt off her knees. The sight of something moving in the corner of her left eye startled her. For a brief moment, it looked like there were many pairs of large sunken eyes embedded in the thick oak trees bordering the estate. She rubbed her eyes and stared back at the woods that stared at her. *Nothing.*

It must be in my head, she assured herself. *Too much sun, if that's possible.*

Helen strolled towards her opulent house, admiring the beauty of the vast gardens. Her father was a dedicated botanist who spared no expense in growing the biggest and most diverse plants on Long Island, which included native and foreign plant species alike, both blooming in brilliant colors in the spring and summer. She stopped next to the sunflower field and breathed in their scent. Closing her eyes to enjoy the aroma, she found she felt connected to the plants around her. Helen preferred their quiet company over the company of people; humans generally annoyed her. This reclusive favor worked out well because her parents were overprotective and never let her venture outside of their rural town.

The sun disappeared behind a thick cloud as thunder rumbled in the sky. Soft raindrops landed on Helen's head and within seconds it started to downpour and so she sprinted towards the front door. Whenever a storm hit, the family's housekeeper Mrs. Cotes had a habit of reminding her that thunder was God's way of letting humanity know that he was angered by their sins.

The family butler, William Crawley, opened the door and greeted her. He was a spritely young man with red hair and a long face. Mr. Crawley hardly ever missed answering someone's call at the front door, even if they hadn't yet called out to him. His family had served the Rains family for generations.

"Just in time, Miss Rains," he said, shutting the door behind her. "Sir Walter warned us of the storm. He said it will get worse before it is better. Shall I bring you some tea, Miss?"

"No thank you, Crawley," Helen said with a smile as she shook her curly red hair dry. "Is father still in the greenhouse?" Though she asked, she already knew the answer – Dr. Rains was always in his greenhouse.

"Indeed, Miss Rains. He's been in there all day," Mr. Crawley replied.

"Not surprising."

Like Helen, Dr. Rains preferred the company of plants over humans. But beyond their mutual passion for vegetation, the two weren't much alike. Helen was sensitive and had an overall cheerful disposition. She enjoyed living in the moment and the little things in life like soaking up the sunshine. Dr. Rains was a selfish and callous man who showed love only for his work and made little time for his family. With a perpetually tense visage, he seemed burdened by something dreadful – something he never spoke about, at least not to Helen. Indeed, he hardly ever had much to say to her, except when it involved his projects; and although she was used to this odd relationship with her father, it still very much upset her.

Helen made her way upstairs and entered her large, quiet room decorated with various plants that reached towards the windows. She peered at the distant forest through her western-facing window. The woods where she thought she had seen those eyes now looked dark and gloomy within, as if the storm clouds had laid an ominous black pall over them; but there were no eyes to be seen. She considered mentioning her strange vision to her parents, but they'd call her mentally unstable. Perhaps she would tell Mrs. Cotes if it still bothered her later; she never judged Helen too harshly, and always made her feel comfortable.

Helen lay down on her soft bed, closed her eyes, and listened to the soothing wind and seemingly endless rain smacking against the roof; the comfort of nature's sounds whisked her into daydreaming. It wasn't long before her reverie was interrupted by a knock at her door.

"Miss Rains," the familiar voice of Mr. Crawley rang out. "Lady Rains requests your presence in the drawing room."

"Ugh," Helen muttered as she returned to reality. She looked at her clock and sighed. It was four o'clock in the afternoon; the usual time her mother Lady Gladys Rains forced her to play the harpsichord. In truth, Helen played the instrument beautifully, and she liked it, but what she didn't care for was being demanded to play it for her mother's amusement nearly every day.

Lady Rains was the exact opposite of her husband. She craved attention and conversation and much preferred the company of others over solitude, and certainly over plants. Indeed, she cared little for plants, although she pretended well when Dr. Rains rambled on about his work. She dutifully listened to his talks, but always admitted to Helen afterwards that she couldn't wait until the subject was changed. She found the entire topic dull.

Helen's mother enjoyed local gossip – who was marrying whom, which families feuded with one another, who was becoming destitute, and the like. She entertained many prominent women each week and they talked for hours about such trivial matters. Much to Helen's chagrin, Lady Rains always invited her to join them. Helen obeyed out of respect, but couldn't wait to break away from the humdrum of the conversations. Oftentimes she had to fight the urge to fall asleep. Such discussions were like torture and so she did not contribute much to them, and took to conversing with herself in her head.

A shared love of music was one of the only things Helen and her mother bonded over, so even though it felt like a chore, she dragged herself out of her room and ventured downstairs to the drawing room. Lady Rains was waiting for her on the sofa, dressed in ruby and sipping red wine.

"There you are, darling," she said cheerfully while rubbing her slender index finger around the rim of the wine glass. "Will you play me some Vivaldi tonight?"

"Sure, mother," Helen said without enthusiasm as she sat down at the harpsichord, setting her slim fingers to the keys and beginning to play. Just like she did during the storm, she fell into a state of pensiveness, this time taken away by the sweet sounds of her instrument. For a few moments, she forgot all about her attention-starved mother sipping her drink on the sofa.

Suddenly they heard the opening of the front

door. Dr. Rains came into the house and effectively ended Helen's tranquility and Lady Rain's enjoyment. Mr. Crawley ran to him and helped take off his rain-soaked lab coat. Dr. Rains was muttering things under his breath that Helen couldn't understand from the drawing room, but she gathered that he was frustrated – as usual.

"Come in, dear," Lady Rains called. "Helen was just entertaining me with such beauteous tones. She gets better every day."

Dr. Rains ignored her comment and made his way to the drawing room. "Has Sir Brewer prepared dinner? I'm famished."

Lady Rains sighed. "How should I know? Like I said, I've been listening to Helen play." Lady Rains shot an appreciative smile at her daughter which was quickly reciprocated.

"Good afternoon, Father," Helen started, "or shall I say good evening? I've always thought the delineation between the two was rather up for debate." Helen smirked as Lady Rains let out a slight chuckle.

"Hello, Helen," her father dryly said. And that was it.

There were some seconds of quiet, save for the sounds of Lady Rains sipping her wine. Finally, Mrs. Cotes entered the room and announced that dinner was set for them in the dining room. Helen enjoyed the tasty meat and vegetable soup, but dinner was no different than any other night. The family sat in silence, and once Dr. Rains was finished, he got up and went upstairs to his study. He shut the door behind him and, like every night, would remain there until the late hours. Dr. Rains wrote profusely, filling notebooks with daily details about his experiments. A few times in the past, Helen snuck into the room and tried to read his papers, but had difficulty understanding her father's sloppy handwriting and learned little from them.

After dinner, Helen went to the drawing room and sat on the sofa. She leaned over to the end table and picked up her book, Charles Darwin's *On the Origin of Species*. It was one of her favorite works, even though she had only read about half of it so far. Darwin's theory of natural selection fascinated her. For about an hour, she explored the world of natural science through Darwin's words. She loved reading after dinner because then she was usually undisturbed by her mother. Her eyelids soon grew heavy and she retired to bed.

Helen didn't stay asleep long. Although she had brushed thoughts of the forest's eyes aside while awake, her slumbering mind led her to the dreadful scene once more. She had a horrible nightmare where she found herself unable to speak in the middle of the dark wood. Then she saw them: The sunken, bloodshot yellow eyes embedded in the thick oak trees, darting in every direction until, all at once, they leered at her. She tried to scream, but could not. Fear-induced paralysis prohibited her from fleeing. Columns of dirt shot up around her ankles and pulled her downward. Just before her head was swallowed underground, she awoke in a sweat.

A dark figure was shaking her. "Wake up, Miss Rains! Wake up!" Mrs. Cote's familiar voice rang out to her.

Helen's heart was beating fast. Her body slowly adjusted from the dream world to the real world. "Mrs. Cotes..." she answered in a haze.

"Yes dear, it's me. You were having a nightmare. I heard your screams from beyond the hall." Mrs. Cotes propped Helen up in bed.

"Thank goodness for you." Helen smiled, glad that the nightmare was just that. "It was horrible. I dreamt that...well..." Helen paused. Doubt as to whether or not she wanted to inform Mrs. Cotes about what she saw earlier crept in. "Nevermind. You're going to think that I'm crazy."

Mrs. Cotes chuckled, rubbing her back. "Oh, go on, dear."

"In my dream, I saw something that I spotted earlier in the forest. There were great yellow eyes...in the trees. I'm sure it was a figment of my imagination, but this dream felt so real, and now I'm second-guessing myself. This was real...real and scary." Helen put her face in the palms of her hands.

Mrs. Cotes stopped rubbing Helen's back. "You saw...what?"

"Eyes in the forest," Helen replied. "I know it sounds mad."

Mrs. Cotes brushed Helen's hair out of her face and flashed a smile. It seemed like a fake smile, but there was no reason for Mrs. Cotes to be fake, not to Helen. "The teenage mind is a wild place, dear. You're growing up so fast that sometimes it's hard to truly understand what's around you. Rest assured, you saw no such thing. No eyes. Indeed, stay away from that forest, dear. It's no place for a proper lady."

Helen wasn't completely satisfied with Mrs. Cotes's words of comfort, but that was that. No point in fishing for words of solace at three o'clock in the morning.

Mrs. Cotes rose from Helen's bedside. "I brought you some water; it's on your nightstand."

Helen grabbed the water and drank it down. "Thank you, Mrs. Cotes. Another glass, please."

"Of course, dear." The housekeeper left the room. After she brought back the water and took her leave, Helen forced herself to return to sleep, and the rest was uneasy.

Helen awoke around seven o'clock in the morning exhausted, but got out of bed and drew the curtains. The warm light bathing the room in yellow perked her up. She got dressed, went downstairs, and had breakfast with her mother. Dr. Rains had missed breakfast and was already in his greenhouse. Helen wondered if he ever slept. After breakfast, she went out into the garden, just as she did the day before.

Helen felt energetic again after a few hours of gardening. She loved dirtying her hands with loose ground. She had almost forgotten about the eyes in the woods until she heard a sound that shattered her serenity.

A blood-curdling scream!

It was loud, drawn out, and ended in a gargled moan – a groan of pain. There was no doubt about the direction from where it came: the forest.

Helen's heart skipped a beat as she looked to the trees and saw the eyes. Those wretched, staring eyes! Her mind raced. She couldn't keep it from her parents anymore. In a panic, Helen ran over to her father's greenhouse.

"Father! Father!" she yelled as she dashed across the lawn.

She came to her father's greenhouse and, despite her fears, marveled at the ornate beauty of the iron and glass structure. She loved the greenhouse, but was hardly ever allowed in it. She recently snuck in when Dr. Rains wasn't home and admired the growing plants in all their summer majesty: vibrant hollyhocks, ivy-leaf geraniums, violets, and more grew among young trees consisting of white and red oaks, red maples, and various spruces and elms. Soil was everywhere, in buckets, bags, or heaped in piles. Burners, test tubes, racks of filled and unfilled vials and beakers, a microscope, and other apparatus were set on tables amid the botanic splendor.

Dr. Rains emerged from the greenhouse looking frustrated. "What madness plagues you, Helen?" His wavy brown hair was wet with sweat that dripped over his dirty face. He had an empty beaker stained with the remnants of some thick green liquid in his hand; his lab coat was blotched with green and brown.

"Screaming eyes!" was all that Helen could initially muster. The strange eyes, her nightmare, and now the screams were too much for her to handle. She took a deep breath. "I saw screaming eyes in the forest!"

Dr. Rains squinted and gave her a peculiar look.

Helen wasn't in the mood. "Father, I am not daft, I know what I saw! There were big eyes in the forest, and they *just* wailed. Did you not hear it?!" Helen put her hands crossly on her hips. She waited with wide eyes for her father's answer.

Dr. Rains sighed. "No, daughter, I did not." He shook his head and rubbed the bridge of his nose. "I suggest you go inside and rest. Mrs. Cotes informed me that you didn't sleep well last night."

As usual, Dr. Rains didn't take Helen seriously and dismissed her concerns. *Why did I think it would have been any different this time?* she thought to herself as she fumed, unsure of what to say next. He wouldn't care if she told him her sleeplessness was the result of a nightmare about the eyes, so she stayed silent.

Dr. Rains grew impatient. "I have work to do. Go inside, young lady. That's not a request."

Inside, Helen continued to fume. *Ugh! I'm sixteen years old for goodness' sake. He cannot demand me anymore!* She wanted to speak her mind to her father, to tell him how she really felt about his insensitive ways. But her hands were shaking and her mind was still processing that god-awful scream. She knew that her quest for information wasn't over, but instead of putting up a fight, Helen just put her head down and consented to go inside.

Dr. Rains flashed an awkward half smile for her obedience and returned to the greenhouse.

Helen seethed with rage as she pushed through the front door. She was sick of feeling emotionally rejected by her father. Mr. Crawley greeted her as she trampled through the house but she ignored him. She wasn't in the mood for chit-chat and felt truly alone. She went into her room and shut the

THE TRIALS OF DR. RAINS

door behind her.

I know what I heard. The forest screamed. My nightmare. The eyes. Perhaps I didn't make it up at all. Perhaps the forest really is alive, Helen thought. She sat on the edge of her bed and stared at the wall. After an hour of stewing in silent discontentment, she was called down for dinner. Although she wasn't in the mood anyway, she thought it odd that her mother hadn't called her down to play the harpsichord. That was the first night in weeks that Lady Rains didn't request music. *Oh well*. In her current fragile emotional state, Helen was relieved that she didn't have to entertain her mother.

A deafening silence dominated dinner, making it more unpleasant than usual. Lady Rains, who tried to keep some semblance of a conversation flowing, looked down at her wine, heartily sipped it, and repeated the process until she started to wobble in her seat. Dr. Rains ate slowly and was very grim. The servants looked troubled, especially Mr. Crawley and Mrs. Cotes. Helen felt numb; she was dealing with her own internal struggles trying to figure out what had the entire house lost in a black cloud. She ate well but didn't enjoy her food. At last, her father broke the uncomfortable quiet.

"You are no longer permitted to leave this house, Helen. Your mother and I have talked it over, and we have deemed that it is for the best."

Helen's heart skipped a beat. "What?" It was like someone just shattered a glass vase on the table. She knew what he had said, but she didn't understand why he said it. *What did I do that was so wrong?!* Her mind started racing.

"Mrs. Cotes told us about your nightmare."

Oh, so you do care? You have a horrible way of showing it.

"Eyes in the forest? Really Helen? And today, you run like a lunatic to my greenhouse, spewing nonsense about screaming trees. Perhaps you've had too much sun lately. You need to rest until we deem you're fit to return outside to your daily routine."

Lady Rains looked at her absently with a touch of sympathy. "I'm sorry, dear, but your father is right." Her tone was one of a defeated person.

Helen's eyes welled up with tears as she stood from the table. Nobody was on her side. Nobody understood her or truly supported her. She ran upstairs, slammed her door shut, and wept.

Helen spent the rest of the night in her room feeling sorry for herself. Of course, her parents didn't bother to see how she was doing, but even Mr. Crawley and Mrs. Cotes stayed away. She tried to cheer herself up by reminding herself that she was the daughter of a wealthy family and didn't have to want for food and shelter. She knew of people in town that were far worse off than she. Lady Rains talked about those kinds of people often. Still, this recent verdict from her parents felt different. It felt final.

Around midnight, Helen tried to soothe herself to sleep, but her mind resisted. She tossed and turned, pulled the covers up to her chin, and threw them down again. Nothing worked. She repeatedly snapped out of sleep at the last moment, just as the realms of waking and sleeping became blurred.

THE TRIALS OF DR. RAINS

Every time she awoke, she thought of the eyes in the trees. At three-thirty in the morning, while her mind languished in a twilight state, Helen was jolted out of bed by the sound of an anguished wail. She pulled open her curtains and stared outside towards the forest. She knew what she had to do, and she would have no rest until she did it – she had to find out what lived in the woods, and her parents' new rule wasn't going to stop her.

She slipped on her shoes and a jacket and quietly made her way downstairs, being careful not to make the steps creak too much. She made it downstairs and secured a kerosene lamp to light her way. When she slowly opened the front door, a gust of fresh warm air rushed into the house. Her messy hair blew about her face. Helen took a deep breath, stepped outside, and gently closed the door behind her.

Her light shoes got wet on the damp grass, but she didn't care. *Whatever my punishment will be for disobeying my parents, it's worth it.* She was rather proud of herself, not only for breaking her parents' rule but also for having the courage to venture outside in the dark at such a late hour.

She stopped short at the border between the estate and the woods. The trees sighed as high winds ripped through their branches. She held the lamp up in front of her. The forest looked utterly black. Pesky mosquitoes were the only creatures that stirred. She continuously swatted at them as they buzzed near her face.

"The time has come, Helen," she said to herself. "You can do this." She crossed the borderline and stood firmly in the gloom of the woods. Just as she did, a deep voice bellowed from somewhere in the darkness.

"Helen," the eerie voice said. "Helen, come to us."

"Who... who are you?!"

"Helen, help us," a higher voice rang out.

Then another: "Help us, Helen. We will not harm you."

"We are a part of you, Helen. Help us."

Helen followed the voices deeper into the woods. With every step she grew more anxious, and the desire to abandon this insane mission crossed her mind more than once. If she just turned around and headed back to bed, she could force herself to sleep. But then her parents would win. No. She had to continue on. She needed to find out why they forbade her from going outside. Sweat dripped from her brow, matting her hair to her freckled face.

"Help us!" they all called out in chilling unison.

She pursued the voices until at last she came to a small circular clearing. Oak trees of various thicknesses lined the outer rim of the circle. Helen squinted in the faint light of the lamp. The black soil at the bottom of the trees looked somewhat fresh, and each tree had colored string around it. Helen realized that these trees did not naturally sprout there. They looked like they were planted by a person.

Suddenly, the trees around the circular clearing opened their bulging yellow eyes at once. They were tinged with red and embedded in the bark. The light from the lamp danced in their deep and sorrowful pupils.

Helen screamed. She tried to control her fear. "What *are* you?!"

The eyes of the trees stared at her without blinking.

A voice rang clearer now, but the voice was in her head. The trees had no mouths. "We are your blood, Helen. Run. Run while you still can."

"What are you talking about?" At that very moment, all of the trees around her let out a tortured scream. It was that same heart-wrenching scream she had already heard twice, only now there were a number of voices screaming at once.

"He comes!" they yelled.

Helen shrieked in fright and dropped the lamp. She'd had enough of this hellish place. When she turned to run she tripped on a thick root that jutted out of the ground. Her body hit the dirt with a thud.

"Ouch!" She cut her right knee on a sharp rock, but couldn't see how bad it was; she felt the blood oozing down her leg. The trees stopped screaming, but their eyes still stared at her. As she sat up, she caught a glimpse of her wounded knee. "No. It cannot be," she said. She grabbed the lamp and pulled it closer to her wounded knee. Her blood was viscous like oatmeal, but that wasn't the most disturbing part. Her blood was green!

Helen's mind raced again. "This must be a nightmare," she said as she tried to wake up. She pinched herself, but to no avail. This was no dream. She let out another horrified scream, and as she did the trees joined her. The surrounding darkness engulfed her.

Before she could compose herself, a man approached her. Fear gripped her as he came closer.

"Helen!" the sharp familiar voice of her father rang out.

Although she wasn't too happy with her father at the moment, she felt relieved. "I'm here! Help me!"

Dr. Rains made his way into the circle and knelt down next to Helen. "You're hurt," he said, but his voice was void of any sense of urgency, and he didn't say a word about the color of her blood. He took a washcloth from his back pocket.

"Father, something is wrong with my blood," Helen said in a panic.

"Hush, child," he said, as he put a moist washcloth over her wound and gently rubbed it over her cut. It burned. "I know."

"You know?"

She started feeling woozy and sleepy. "But… I… I don't…"

"Rest now, Helen. Hush, hush. You'll be well soon."

Just before Helen blacked out, she saw him smile.

Helen awoke in a haze to the sound of her parents' voices, but was unable to understand their words. Her body was numb and her vision was blurred, but judging by the intense heat around her, she could tell that she was in the greenhouse. In her daze, she couldn't recollect what had happened.

Her parents' voices gradually became clearer,

as she struggled to break free from her condition. She noticed her mother was sobbing.

"I wish it hadn't come to this, Walter," Lady Rains said. "She was such a wonderful harpsichord player, and kept me company when my friends were unavailable."

"I know, Gladys. But we knew the risks of growing a teenager. They are too stubborn and inquisitive, too aware of their surroundings. She never would have stopped until she blew the lid off of my entire operation, and I'd be ruined," Dr. Rains replied with a hint of sadness.

Lady Rains gently rested her hand on the trunk of a freshly-planted oak tree in a large pot. "I suppose you'll have to try a younger child next time," she said in between her sobs.

Helen felt a hand resting on her, as if in sympathy. She tried to yell but no words came out. She tried to squirm but found that she could not move. She was as stiff as a tree.

"How could I have foreseen that her siblings would manifest eyes and voices after I planted them?" her father asked. "It's an unfortunate yet fascinating consequence. No doubt, Helen will grow the same features soon enough."

Suddenly, a blood-curdling scream shot out from the young oak tree. Helen's parents jumped, but Dr. Rains quickly composed himself and chuckled.

"See that, dear? Helen is already using her voice, and she hasn't even been planted a month yet! I think I'll keep her in the greenhouse for a few more weeks before moving her into the forest with the other failed experiments."

"The forest?" Lady Rains worriedly asked. "No, Walter, not there. Helen was special, and I'd like to visit her. Can she stay in the greenhouse?"

"Well, alright, dear," Dr. Rains said as he ushered his wife towards the door. "We'll keep her here until she grows too tall."

Helen hopelessly screamed again and again.

UNHALLOWED EVENING
by R.C. Mulhare

On Halloween night, most people went to parties or stayed home to hand out offerings to the ghosts and goblins at the door; that is, if they weren't shepherding their own little monsters about the more well-lit neighborhoods of East Manuxet. I, on the other hand, pulled up before a house near a graveyard to resurrect my dead husband.

No, he isn't a zombie; we hadn't buried him there. I wasn't calling on a robed necromancer or a medium dressed like a Viennese operetta fortune teller to aide me in calling up his ghost – unless you consider medical scientists the modern necromancers.

I parked my car in the drive of the old gambrel-roofed house near the East Manuxet Cemetery, the dwelling previously occupied by generations of caretakers and their families or protégés. After killing the ignition, I sat there for a long time with my hands on the steering wheel. *Danni, you sure that you want to do this?* I asked myself. Yes, this was what Mal wanted, and I was fulfilling a desire he'd had, a promise, as it were, that we'd made. He'd wanted to donate himself to science, and in particular, the science of a friend of ours who, in his words, sought a cure for the common death. Mal had an accident while trimming tree branches on Victor's property, and I'd wondered in the ensuing days if it had been quite as accidental as we thought.

At length, I opened the car door, got out, and took out the box of ritual tools I thought necessary to bring along. Locking the doors against older imps with more devious intentions than soaping windows or toilet papering hedges, I hoisted the box and walked up the flagstone path to the front door. The New England night wind skittered frost-crisped leaves across my path; the willow and hemlock tops swayed along the stone wall between the cemetery and the caretaker's property Victor had left the porch and upstairs unlit to keep the goblins away. He'd also made some effort to cover the basement windows. Not thoroughly, since you could see light around some of the curtains. I knocked on the front door. Realizing he might not hear me, I hit the glowing buzzer.

I heard nothing for a few moments. I hit the buzzer harder and longer. Finally I heard footsteps approaching inside. The lock rattled and the door swung open on the security chain.

Victor peered out around the edge, one of his blue eyes glaring at me half over, half through one lens of his eyeglasses. "I've told you a dozen times, I'm not interested in talking about your Lord and Savior Jesus -" He paused, glancing away to recover his composure, and took the door off the chain. "Danni, I'm sorry. I've had door-to-door Bible salesmen here all week. I swear

Halloween brings *them* and not ghosts out of the woodwork."

"I'm sorry if I'm late," I said. "I got cold feet, but I'm better now."

"No worries, you're on time." He stepped back and pulled the door open. I stepped through and he eyed the box, curiously.

"You could say I brought a few props, to draw in Mal's spirit."

He narrowed his eyes, shutting the door behind me. "If it helps you feel better about the procedure..." He sounded dubious, but wisely let that sentence trail off, not expressing his usual skepticism, as he did with most people.

Since high school when the three of us started hanging together, he'd been the blunt critic of anything that couldn't be quantified, but he'd mellowed toward me after the accident that claimed Mal's body. I don't know if that came from concern for me or to avoid offending me and risking the chance that I didn't agree to his experiments; it could have been some combination of both, but I could live with it.

He beckoned me to follow him through the sparsely-furnished front room, down a short hallway to the basement door, then downstairs. There was a clean area rigged with thick plastic sheeting in the main section of the basement. Behind the plastic walls, what looked like a large fish tank full of orange-tinged fluid stood on a table against the back wall, while a surgical table dominated the center of the room. Set against another wall were two heart-lung machines pumping away, the connected tubes on one carrying blood to the giant fish tank. The tubes from the other connected to a series of smaller tanks, most containing back-up organs, while the largest of this group contained Mal's head, gently floating in the solution. I tried not to think too hard about where Victor had procured any of his specimens. His work in the pathology lab of Manuxet Medical Center put him in contact with a lot of materials. A shadowed form like a human body lay in the depths of the larger tank.

I set the box on a table close to the clean area, then took out the items I had deemed essential to the experiment – battery candles, an album of photos, a journal I'd kept since the accident, one of Mal's favorite tee shirts and a pair of his cargo pants, a bottle of scorch, a box of his favorite Chinese takeout and an MP3 player and its dock – and arranged them on the table.

Victor glanced at the altar, honing his gaze onto the candles. "Mood lighting?"

"It's a bit like a Dia de Muertos altar," I admitted.

"Except we're bringing someone back to life, rather than honoring the dead," Victor said. He didn't say "if this works", but his tone hinted that he'd thought as much, bracing himself for any possible outcome.

I turned back to the work area, when something buzzed overhead. We looked at each other. "It's the doorbell. I put a second buzzer down here," he explained, frowning in annoyance. "But who the hell is it at this hour?"

"It's Halloween. Want me to send the goblins on their way?"

"Please do." He turned back to the largest tank while pulling on a pair of shoulder-high rubberized gloves and reaching in.

I hurried up the stairs, the buzzer resounding again. I rooted in the kitchen cupboards, looking for anything to placate the spooks, found a large box of trail mix bars (Victor always tried to get by on the least amount of food imaginable) and dumped them into a plastic mixing bowl. I ran for the door, hoping my ankle-length black dress and black boots made me look like a modern witch.

Outside, I found a toddler dressed as a puppy, a six-year-old girl dressed as a pixie, a bored-looking teen-aged girl wearing goth attire I suspected she couldn't wear to school, and a bed-sheet ghost too tall to be anything but their mischievous dad or mom. "Trick or treat!" the kids chorused. Teen Goth sighed and the ghost moaned a cheery "Woo-woo wooooo"

"Aren't you adorable?" I chirped, holding out the bowl. "Wish I had more, but it's been busy."

"Figures, you're near the cemetery," Teen Goth said, grabbing a granola and stuffing it into the black pillowcase she carried, while Pixie took one with delicate fingertips and Puppy tried to grab at the bowl with paw-mitt covered hands.

"Is it true?" Teen Goth asked. "Does a mad scientist live here? Does he experiment on the stiffs in the graveyard?" She jolted, glaring up at the ghost, who shook its head; I gathered Papa Ghost poked her in the ankle as a warning.

"Well, a scientist lives here, but he works at Manuxet Medical, so not much time for experiments," I replied.

UNHALLOWED EVENING

Teen Goth's blank frown got more bored. "Lame. I figured Kenny was bullshitting me."

"You're supposed to say bull shoes," Pixie said, poking her sister with her wand, as Papa Ghost herded them away.

I went inside, dropping the bowl onto the dusty sideboard in the front room and returning downstairs.

Victor pulled the larger segment of his creation halfway out of its tank; it hung in a sling strung from a pulley system jerry-rigged from the beams overhead, and now puttered with the tubes sticking out of the neck. I tried not to think where he'd acquired it: the pieces in the other tanks hinted at the origins of this body, or its materials. "Goblins at the door as we suspected?" he asked, not looking up.

"Yeah, two cute munchkins, their bored goth sister and their bed-sheet ghost dad." From the questions Teen Goth asked, I take it you're a local legend. She asked if a mad scientist lives here."

"I've suspected the kids tell stories about me. I haven't kept my profession a secret."

"You haven't told people what you do when you're not working pathology at Manuxet Medical, have you? Because she wanted to know if you're the local Doctor Frankenstein."

He emitted a half-cough, half-laugh sound. "Of course not. They wouldn't believe it if I told them Do you really think I'd volunteer that information? And I'm the mad one?"

Finding a gown and pulling it out, I asked with a smirk, "Do you think of yourself as a mad scientist?"

He looked over his shoulder and said with mock profundity and a finger in the air. "It's said that genius and madness walk a close fine line, and I'd never call myself 'normal', just misunderstood."

The buzzer went off again. "Please get that, will you?" he asked in exasperation.

"I found some energy bars in your cupboard: they held off the first batch, we'll see if it works on the rest of the dark forces" I said, setting aside the gown and heading upstairs.

On the doorstep, I found some teenagers and a middle school kid, one dressed as a hockey player, his mask on his head and rollerblades on his feet with his candy pail tied to his hockey stick, another dressed as a Ghostbuster with a homemade proton pack, two kids wearing horror clown masks with sweatshirts and sweatpants, and the middle school kid with a Frankenstein's monster mask.

"Energy bars?" the hockey kid, who appeared to be the leader, said, eyeing the bowl. "Lame."

"Sorry for the short supply. It's been busy," I said, going by the seat of my pants.

"Are there really zombies living in the basement here?" one horror clown asked.

Frankenstein's monster grabbed two bars. "Jake, zombies don't *live*."

"Well, they don't *die*, either unless you boom-stick their heads," Other Horror Clown said.

"Well, maybe they are *dead* around here," Horror Clown One offered.

"Nope, no zombies here," I said, though this chatter twigged something in my head. "Just me and a friend who lives here."

"Oh, having a private party?" Ghostbuster asked, in a wink-wink, nudge-nudge way. Frankenstein's monster whacked him upside the head.

"Nah, just chilling and watching movies in between visitors," I said.

They went away arguing whether or not they should check out the cemetery, while Ghostbuster wondered out loud about what he'd see if he peeked into the window, which made Hockey Guy whack him in the back with his stick.

By the time I retreated downstairs, Victor had the head raised from the tank in a smaller sling similar to the one holding the body, still linked to the heart-lung machine. I got down in time to watch him insert an IV into the neck of the head… Mal's head.

"Saline drip?"

"He's going to need that and glucose on top of the serum he's been bathing in," Victor said. "For that matter, it's time we weaned the head and the body off the serum, though I might have to give him a booster shot every day till he's healed up."

"I can take care of that: I helped my grandfather with his insulin shots, toward the end. What's in it anyway? I know I've asked, but could you refresh my memory?"

He smirked at me. "I'd tell you, but I'd have to kill you and use you as a test subject." He paused, growing serious. "It's something I found in a medical school library in Salem, some notes from back in the 1920s."

"And it didn't work back then?"

"Mostly because the scientist didn't have the technology we have now to keep his subjects alive."

"Time to put him together?"

"The time's come." Victor pulled on some cords that moved the body to the surgical table and lowered it onto the tabletop.

He'd gotten the head into place and lowered it close to the body, when the door buzzer went off again.

"That does it," Victor muttered.

"Maybe we should shut that off for the rest of the night."

Dropping the tubes he held, he shucked out of his surgical gown, dropped it onto a table, ducked out of the clean area to a small laundry cart, dug out a blood-splattered shirt and pulled it on.

"What the...Victor, what are you doing? Do I want to know how you got your shirt all bloody?"

Stalking back into the clean area, he peered over his shoulder and reaching into one of the tanks, took out a foot, unhooked it from the heart-lung machine, and hauled it out. "You really don't want to know." He stalked out of the room and upstairs, his back ramrod straight.

"Victor, get down here!" I ran after him, in case I had to talk him out of a mess.

By the time I caught up, Victor had a hand on the door latch, the buzzer chirr-ing again, accompanied by a muffled chorus of "Trick or Treat" outside. I reached for Victor's arm, when

UNHALLOWED EVENING

he flung open the door, his free hand gripping the foot by its ankle. Outside stood a cluster of college-kid goblins: I glimpsed one in full Freddy Kruger gear (hat, mask, shirt, even the glove, which looked like a lovingly-made high school shop project), a black kid in a long black coat with a velvet collar and a hook sticking out of one sleeve, a heavy-set kid in a white full-face hockey mask and wielding a rubber machete, a very tall, skinny personage in a black suit with a blank white mask, and one short, dark-haired kid with glasses in a black suit, carrying a 100cc syringe full of glow-stick fluid.

"Ah, new test subjects," Victor drawled. The slasher kids screamed and yawped before bolting out of sight, heading toward the cemetery.

Except Syringe Guy, who stared at the foot. "Excellent prop, very life-like. Where'd you find that?"

"I know where I can get them wholesale." Victor slammed the door in the kid's face before stalking back downstairs.

Once down there, he dropped the foot back into the tank, hooked it back to the heart-lung machine, dried his hands on a towel, shucked off the bloodied shirt and going to one corner of the work area, reached up to yank a wire loose from the buzzer box.

"Looks you had a fan back there, though you scared his friends good."

"Meaning I only partly succeeded."

"Well, half a loaf's better than no soup at all."

Victor looked at me, his eyes softening. "Didn't Mal used to say that?"

I looked toward the surgical slab. "Maybe he'll say it again soon."

He set to work in earnest; we had no further interruptions. While he set up the surgical tools, I went upstairs to have a look at the clean room he'd set up there, careful not to touch anything. The grafts would require Mal to take immuno-suppressants for some time after the surgery, which would require keeping him in a clean area till his new body and his head accepted each other. It would make life a little tricky, with him having to stay here, but I'd grown accustomed to shuttling back and forth to Victor's house. I went downstairs and switched on the MP3 player, queuing up a playlist of Mal's favorite songs: soft rock, classic rock and soundtracks of movies we'd seen and enjoyed together. "Time I'd better start setting the mood to attract or awaken his spirit."

Victor glanced at me through the curtain, a skeptical pucker under the edge of his surgical cap and the headlamp strapped to his forehead. His surgical mask muffled his voice as he spoke. "I suppose that could go either way: it will help him remember things, or it won't."

"Oh ye of little faith," I said with a playful smile.

He leveled a look at me, then snorted under his mask and turned back to his work. "I'd substitute 'certainty' or 'confidence' for 'faith', but that would eviscerate that quote."

I suited up in the surgical gown and entered the clean area. He'd started to attach the head by the time I got back. "How is he?"

UNHALLOWED EVENING

"I've got the spine attached, but don't expect him to get up and tango any time soon," he said, without looking up from stitching muscle tissue to the sides of the neck, filling the void between the surgical cut on Mal's neck and a similar one on the body.

Time passed. Victor worked steadily, his small hands deft as he knit his friend, my lover back together. I helped by handing him the tools as he needed them, though at one point, I ducked out to queue up another playlist on the MP3 player: recordings I'd made, reading out loud from Mal's and my journals, reliving experiences that he and I – sometimes with Victor accompanying us – had shared.

Evening gave way to midnight. Going back to what I'd learned in nursing school, I cleaned instruments for Victor and loaded out fresh ones for the next phase: attaching the skin to cover the muscle grafts. I paused, resting my hip against a work table, my head bowing as my brain grew sleepy for a moment. I shook myself awake, thinking something from the Talmud that my co-worker Rivekeh had shared with me: God creating one version of Eve while Adam watched, awake and shuddering at bones appearing, organs forming inside the torso, nerves and blood vessels weaving around them, muscle and skin covering it all; of Adam quailing back in fear as this woman approached him, he refusing to accept a woman who had taken form before his very eyes. And here I'd dozed for a moment through the work of the physician not so divine, piecing my spouse together, on this night when people traditionally took a good hard stare at the things that scare them and responded with a laugh, even a nervous one.

"Are you ready?" I asked.

Victor still carefully stitched at the skin covering Mal's neck. "Almost: give it a few moments and we'll be ready to give it the spark of life."

"A kite in a lightning storm?" I asked, thinking of the Halloween when Mal dragged us both to a marathon of Universal's Frankenstein movies, at an old-time movie theater in Salem.

Victor glared, then laughed, gently. "Close: I've had some success when I've applied a defibrillator to the heart." Once he'd finished applying the skin grafts, he put the head and neck into a cervical halo, the kind used to stabilize severe neck injuries, but he'd added a few modifications for this specific case. He took a hospital gown from a drawer in one of the tables and started draping it over the body, intending to dress it, but I cut in. "Let me do this, it's my place." Taking the gown from him, I draped it over the body, sliding the arms into the sleeves and with Victor's help raising him, folded it under the back.

Once we had him covered, we moved the body to a teeter-board in the far corner, setting it rocking for several minutes, encouraging the blood to flow in the veins. Stabilizing the board again, Victor brought over a defibrillator, charged it and applied the paddles. It doesn't appear as dramatic as the TV medical shows make it look: the body doesn't jolt up from the table, though it twitches a bit. Victor charged the device again; the body twitched again and the chest rose as it drew in a breath.

Mal, I had to think of him as Mal, moaned in the back of his throat. "Mal?" I said, stepping closer. "Mal, are you there?

The eyelids fluttered open, the eyes rolling side to side but not focusing on anything. "Malcolm, can you hear us?" Victor asked.

"Duh... Dan-nee..?" Mal said, trying to turn his head but unable to because of the halo.

"Yes, yes, it's me." I ignored the tears starting in my eyes. "I'm right here. I waited for this day. I've worked with Victor to bring you back to me – back to us."

He shifted stiffly, trying to sit up, but could not. Between Victor and I, we lifted Mal onto a stretcher, a basin of supplies at his feet, carrying him up the stairs to the clean room. We laid Mal on the bed, Victor supporting his torso, I supporting his legs. Victor propped Mal's shoulders with pillows, then hung up two intravenous bags from a pole by the bedside, one of a glucose-saline mix, the other of antihistamines and other drugs to prevent tissue rejection.

"What... day?" Mal croaked.

I knelt by the bed. "It's Halloween, a month after the accident. You remember our plan, in case anything happened to either of us."

"My... head?" he asked.

"Yes, Victor did it: he put together a body for you after your accident. We – he – attached your head tonight." I reached between the plastic curtains that surrounded the bed, and with my gloved hand, found one of Mal's hands – now that I could call them his hands, now that his nerves had found a way to connect to them. His fingers, still cool but growing slowly warmer even as I held them, closed on mine, almost like a newborn baby would grasp someone's fingertip. "Can you remember what happened?"

He twitched his head as if he wanted to move it, but the halo prevented him. "No, nothing...pain...darkness."

"What about...what about anything...beyond this world?"

"Hos...pital smells...clean...warm...damp...dark..." he managed.

"Dark?"

"Still dark...here..." Mal replied.

"He might be suffering some amount of sensory loss," Victor said, concerned.

"It's all right; I'm right next to you." I pressed Mal's hand. "We're in Victor's house. He set up a recovery room for you."

"Recovery...good...still too dark..." Mal said, rolling his eyes aimlessly. He stiffened, eyes widening and darting about, seeking the cause of his fear. "No..." he moaned, looking toward me, staring through me rather than at me. "No...get it away..."

"It's all right." I pressed his hand. He jerked away as if my touch burned him.

"The dark...the darkness...something in the darkness..." Mal said. He sat up, stiff-limbed. Victor tried to push him back onto the pillows, but

Mal pushed him aside, fumbling at the halo, as if to pry it off.

"Malcolm, lay down, you're still healing," I said, reaching for him.

"Try and contain him; I got sedatives in case this happened," Victor said, taking a syringe and a bottle from the tray and filling it quickly. Victor reached for Mal's arm as I tried to press Mal down, hands on his shoulders. Mal batted at me with his free arm, hitting me across the face. He elbowed Victor in the neck, sending him staggering into a wall, hitting his head. Mal slid off the bed, falling to the floor in an awkward heap. I caught him under the arms to help him up, but he twisted free and staggered for the door.

"Malcolm, stay. We're only trying to help you," I pleaded. Mal stared at me with blank eyes, then opened his mouth in a wordless howl that couldn't possibly come from a human voice box. I reached for him, but he bolted blindly from the room.

Victor, recovering, rose and ran after him; I followed them, out into the hallway. Mal staggered into the front room, banging into and bouncing off the walls. Victor grabbed at his arm, but Mal flailed out at him, feeling around till he found the front door and opened it, falling out into the night. Rising, he stumbled across the lawn, still howling, heading for the cemetery.

The kids had gotten busy. So much for going undisturbed by cutting the buzzer. They'd draped the trees with Halloween store crime scene tape and silly string; someone had spray-painted "Dead Inside" on the door. I couldn't linger to survey the wreckage. We had to get Mal back. We ran after him, calling his name. Mal bolted through a gap in the hemlocks, stumbling into a tree. In the process his right arm somehow broke loose from the stitches. I stooped to grab the arm and bring it with us.

"Leave it! We have to keep his spine intact," Victor yelled, following Mal.

I ran after Victor, through the trees, the branches whapping us like the haunted trees in the old *Wizard of Oz* movie. A mist had risen in the cold of the night, flowing among the headstones. I saw lights in the near distance and heard voices chanting: kids partying or holding goofy rituals among the stones.

"Great, kids messing with magick," Victor growled, pausing beside me.

"Don't just stand there, we have to get him back before they see him." I ran toward the lights.

Mal had stumbled into a low-hanging branch of an oak tree, snagging the halo on it. He yanked and bucked wildly, the branches tearing the halo loose before he finally broke free.

The chanting stopped as I got closer. Then someone yelled in fear. I ducked behind a box tomb and crept along behind it toward the firelight, peeking around one corner.

Mal stumbled into the ritual circle of college kids in what looked like their graduation gowns, holding torches around a bonfire. Their ritual master boggled at Mal and dropped his book of spells. Mal staggered toward them, but tripped, falling headfirst into the flames. His gown caught fire and he rose like a human torch, screaming louder. The kids began to yell.

"That's not what we wanted!"

"That isn't the Black Goat of the Forest."

"Who is that?"

"Never mind who. What is that?"

"Oh Yog, it's a zombie! How did you summon a zombie?"

"Get me outta here!"

"I want my mummy!"

The kids then dropped their torches and ran for the cars parked on a lane nearby.

One kid reached his car first, bundling in through an open side window, robes and all, then started the engine. Some of his buddies caught up, yanking doors open as the car jerked into motion. "Why isn't it stopping?" one kid yelled.

"You burn vampires, not zombies," another yelled back.

"Well, how am I supposed to keep it all straight," the first one snapped.

"Enough arguing, just get us outta here!"

Mal staggered towards the cars, falling out into the lane. I ran after him, trying to grab him, but the moving car barreled toward him. He stood as I fell back onto the grass; the car plowed into him, rolling him onto the windshield and over the roof before he rolled down the back. He hit the pavement like a sack of potatoes, battered, the stitches on his neck already breaking. His body started to rise, but his head lolled on the remaining strands and slid loose, hitting the pavement and rolling toward me, coming to rest at my feet.

"Worst case of tissue rejection ever," Victor muttered behind me.

"And that's why you ended up in the East Manuxet Cemetery with Mal's head in your lap?" asked Officer Barbara O'Brien, from across the table in the interrogation room. I sat with my hands huddled in the bloodstained lap of my dress. The wan light of an autumn dawn filtered through the wired glass window above us.

"That's everything," I said. "But those cultist kids..."

"The kids called in what happened. They're facing trespassing charges, but that's a bit beside the point. We get some weird calls on Halloween, but you and Dr. Cornish's experiment and those kids are about the weirdest we've had yet."

"But I'm telling you, we weren't part of that ritual."

"Never said you were, though I wonder if those kids called up something they shouldn't and it got into your husband's head, makin' him spazz out like that."

"You really believe that?" I asked.

"After the things I've seen, I've started to wonder if there's precious little that's impossible, especially on Halloween."

"So what happens to Victor and me?"

"That's for a judge to decide, but the worst for you is probably aiding and abetting in some dodgy and unsanctioned medical experiments. Most of that's on Dr. Cornish's shoulders. I don't take you as the sort to try it again."

I shook my head, tears in my eyes. "No, I just wanted Mal back, but now he's gone for good."

"Let me get you some tissues and coffee."

O'Brien stepped out of the interrogation room, as another officer, Sergeant Rand, her superior, stepped out of another interrogation room across the hall where I suspected they had Victor. The door remained open and I could hear everything that passed between them.

"So what'd she tell you?" Sergeant Rand asked.

"She had a hand in Cornish's work: she signed the head over to him, but she didn't have any malicious intent," O'Brien replied.

"She still aided him, and he's already under suspicion with the medical board."

"Using discards from Manuxet Medical Center?"

"Stolen from recently deceased bodies slated for cremation."

"Talk about recycling and not letting anything go to waste," O'Brien said dryly. Her quip must not have amused her boss, and it certainly didn't amuse me. "Sorry, it's my first time with a case that looks like it came out of an old black and white monster movie. All right, I'd better prep her for her day in court,"

A half hour later, with O'Brien and another officer escorting me and a group of the female college-aged cultists, still in their black and red robes, I emerged from the back of the police station into the November daylight. After the wild night before and the darkness that had engulfed it, the sky overhead never seemed so bright and blue.

The chill in the air never felt more bracing and invigorating, a reminder that I still lived. And yet now, I lived in a world where Mal no longer existed. The experiment had failed. I hadn't been able to keep my promise to Mal, and now Victor and I would pay for trying to realize our hopes.

O'Brien guided me, handcuffed and with shackles hobbling my ankles, toward a van marked "Middlesex County Sheriff's Dept." I looked across the loading area behind the police station, as another group, the male cultist kids, with Victor at the back of the line, emerged, several male officers escorting them to another Sheriff's Department van. Victor carefully avoided looking toward me, but at that distance, I couldn't tell if he looked annoyed or bored or what.

Beyond that van stood another van marked "Middlesex County Coroner's Office". A man and a woman each in dark blue windbreakers emerged from the station, wheeling a gurney on which lay two black treated canvas bags. Victor glanced toward them before the officer closest to him guided him into the back of the prisoner transport, and his eyes widened. The body bags seized against the straps holding it onto the gurney, letting out low, muffled noises, like someone yelling and trying to break loose.

THE MAZE
by K. J. Watson

Hertfordshire, England, 1905.

Certain books can cause extreme fear. With a harrowing use of words and images, these stories can incite our imaginations and access doors in our minds that should never be opened. As a librarian and bibliophile, I have thought about this topic a great deal. Indeed my latest client, Miss Pope, confirmed the effect of such books by owning a volume that was truly repulsive. But I have also found that there is a terror based in reality, a dreadful terror that is far worse than a world conjured by sentences and paragraphs.

My unhappy tale begins with a letter that I received one summer's morning. It read as follows:

Dear Mr.____,

I understand that you organize and catalogue private libraries. I have a collection of books that my late father's family accumulated over many years. These books are in disarray. Frankly, I do not care for them; however, their state of untidiness is another matter. It distresses me.

Consequently, I would be grateful if you would come to my home and accept the commission of putting my library in order.
  Yours faithfully,
  Miss Pope

The task sounded ordinary and was the type of work that formed the basis of my livelihood. Being early summer, the address of Miss Pope's home in the Hertfordshire countryside was also an attractive lure. So I wrote a short note back, accepting the job and confirming my terms.

A week later, I packed a bag and caught a late afternoon train from London to within a few miles of the Pope residence. When I alighted at the station, I hoped to find a carriage waiting for me. Miss Pope knew of my pending arrival and I assumed that even a humble librarian would qualify for private transportation. I was mistaken. I waited several minutes in vain, after which I asked the station's porter for directions. He said nothing in reply, simply pointing towards a lane. I thanked this surly individual and set off.

I advanced confidently between the lane's unkempt stone walls and ancient trees. I saw no reason to be unduly worried by a rural walk. Even with the sun beginning to fade beyond the horizon, the air remained warm and there was ample summer brightness left in the sky.

Despite the pleasant environment, I had not reckoned on continuing for almost an hour without any sign of a dwelling. Finally, the lane stopped before an expanse of coarse grass. I looked for a further track, without success, and was debating whether to turn back when a vast winged shape swooped at me from a nearby tree. In surprise, I ducked, lost my footing and fell, knocking my head on a stone.

I rose groggily, ran my hand across my head and winced at the pain. My fingers were smeared with blood. I knelt to clean them on the grass, and when I stood again, saw a large house several hundred yards away. I must not have seen the property before because of some trick of the evening light.

Although my head was throbbing, I picked up my bag and walked on, assuming that I had reached my destination.

The house was the most unappealing mansion I had ever laid eyes upon. The stonework was uniformly dull gray, while the windows were small with leaded panes. The building's shape was also unimaginative. It was square and plain. There were no bays, battlements or decorative work to relieve the simplicity.

I paused, looking for a way in, and saw what appeared to be the only entrance: a modest wooden door. On my way to approach it, I heard a scream of torment coming from around the side of the house. Clearly someone was in need of help. I dropped my bag, ran round the corner and stopped.

In the shadows of the falling night, I struggled at first to make out what lay in front of me. I then realized that it was an unbroken hedge, twenty or more feet high, stretching from the wall of the house for perhaps quarter of a mile. My way was completely blocked; yet it seemed likely that the scream had originated from behind it for no one was in sight.

I approached the hedge, searching for a way through, walking almost to its end and back again. I could find no way in. The scream had not reoccurred and my head was aching, so I began to think that a wiser course of action was to go to the house, find Miss Pope and inform her of what I had heard. I was about to do just that when a rustle of leaves and stems preceded the sudden arrival of a severe-looking woman dressed in riding clothes and carrying a whip. Bewildered, I stepped back.

"Did you come through the hedge? Did you hear the scream?" I asked, forgetting, in my confusion, to introduce myself.

The woman stared at me. I was disconcerted and tried to hold her gaze, but my eyes would only focus on the scar that stretched from her hairline to the tip of her jaw.

"I'm Miss Pope," the woman said at last, brushing past me. "You, presumably, are the librarian. There was no scream. Come this way."

Miss Pope headed to the front of the house. For a moment I stood still, mouth agape. I then followed, retrieved my bag and caught up with Miss Pope as she waited by the door that I had seen earlier.

"Come in," she instructed.

Miss Pope locked the door behind us and pocketed the key.

We stood in an unadorned hall. Candles burning in plain sconces cast negligible light. My headache now felt worse.

THE MAZE

"I cut my head on a stone on the way here. An owl, I think, surprised me and I fell. Do you have warm water, please, and perhaps a salve for the wound?"

Miss Pope grimaced and pointed at a door.

"That leads to the library."

"Thank you. All the same ..."

Turning and nodding towards another door, Miss Pope said, "This is your room. You'll find everything you need in there. Goodnight."

With that, Miss Pope swiftly extinguished all the candles in the hall except one. She removed this last source of light from its sconce and carried it with her as she left, stranding me in darkness.

I edged forward to where I believed the door to my room was situated and eventually managed to open it. A single flickering candle lit the space that I entered; inside, there were a bed, wardrobe and chest of drawers – on the latter stood a jar of antiseptic ointment. How Miss Pope could have known I would require the ointment perplexed me.

To the side of the wardrobe, an open doorway led to a bathroom. I put down my bag and went in with the candle. Using the ice-cold water from the tap, I carefully washed the back of my head and returned to the bedroom, where I smeared ointment on my wound.

I remember nothing else of that night. I imagine that I was so exhausted, I lay on the bed and fell instantly asleep. What woke me, I believe, was the click of a lock. My first impression was that someone, presumably Miss Pope, was securing me in the room. I hurried to the door and tried the handle. The door opened. It seemed that the noise I had heard was of Miss Pope unlocking it.

I stepped into the hall. Miss Pope was watching me from a corner.

"How is your head?" she asked.

"Good, thank you," I said as I realized that the pounding in my head had considerably eased.

"You will take breakfast and your other meals in your room," she said. "I will bring them to you."

She pointed to a tray resting on a table. The tray had plates of bread and cake alongside butter and jars of preserves. To judge by the cheering smell, there was also a pot of tea.

"One other matter," Miss Pope continued. "Restrict yourself to the library and your room. Do not wander around the house or grounds."

I nodded, thanked her for the breakfast and took the tray into my room. As I ate, I considered what I should do next. I wondered whether the peculiarity of what I had experienced over the past twelve hours or so was a sign that I should terminate my work here before it had begun. Even so, I was keen to see the library before I went; and indeed, when I did, I resolved to stay.

A library is my natural domain, one where I feel most comfortable. Furthermore, I relish disordered shelves, books piled haphazardly on floors and chairs, and the smell of old leather and dust. To me, these clear indications of abandonment are satisfying. For in these conditions, my desire to handle books and classify them comes to the fore. And I have to say that the state of Miss Pope's sizeable library presented me with the gratifying prospect of weeks of labor.

So despite my reservations, I settled into a steady pace of work over the next two days. I was left in peace and saw no one. I could not even look through the windows because the hedge that I had come across that first evening obstructed the view. All I could see was a mass of vivid crimson leaves.

My meals appeared in the hall, delivered, I assumed, by Miss Pope. In the evenings, I sat in the library, reading. And when I retired for the night, I heard the clicks of the locks turning on the library and bedroom doors.

I slept reasonably well. The lesion in the back of my head quickly healed, as far as I could tell. There was certainly no blood smeared on my pillow. When I occasionally woke, I listened for disturbing noises, but the house and its grounds were remarkably silent. As for the scream that I had heard when I arrived, I decided that it was probably the hunting call of the same owl that had caused me to fall.

The books in the library were not especially remarkable. The main subjects were moral philosophy, agriculture, economics and religion. In addition, there were literary novels, tales of adventure and collections of children's stories. Nonetheless, many volumes were first editions and worth preserving.

It was on my third day that I came across the book that stood out from all the others and that I wish I had never encountered. I found it concealed behind several publications on mercantile voyages. The book had no markings on the cover or spine, which was unusual, so I took it to a nearby table and opened it. The first page gave a title—*The Pope Maze*—and the name of the publisher. I knew from experience that this publisher had specialized in private editions with print runs that sometimes consisted of just one book. The date across the bottom of the page was 1693.

The book was a description of a maze to be built here on the grounds of the Pope mansion. The detail was technical and thorough, and referred to existing mazes in various European countries. The proposal for the shrub that should be used for the maze was particularly interesting: *Buxus sempervirens sanguis ruber*, blood-red boxwood. So the hedge outside the library windows was part of a maze. And that large expanse of hedge that I had come across on my arrival was possibly one side of the perimeter.

Something troubled me, though. I am not a horticulturist, yet I was sure that most hedges are generally green. I went to the shelves and removed a book on garden cultivation and management that I remembered from the day before. I thumbed through the pages, looking for an entry that gave details about *Buxus sempervirens* and found one easily enough, although there was no mention of a *sanguis ruber*—blood-red—boxwood variety.

I returned to *The Pope Maze* and continued to read. Oddly, the practical description of the construction of the maze began to degenerate into fanciful nonsense. For instance, the writer talked about a "fusion" between the maze and the house.

THE MAZE

I stopped reading and turned over several pages of text.

It is too late now to say that I should never have turned those pages and that I should simply have returned the book to a shelf. But such a regret is understandable because what I saw made me gasp in alarm. The page open in front of me was covered in crude drawings of appalling human suffering.

I closed my eyes and breathed deeply. I told myself that I needed to view this book dispassionately. I opened my eyes and turned over the rest of the pages. They contained further ghastly images, some of which had faint handwritten comments around them that seemed to be a foreign tongue or gibberish.

My attempt to be unemotional about the book's content failed. I began to feel horribly nauseous in my stomach and bowels. I staggered from the library to my room. Without ceremony, I fell onto the bed as I tried to drive from my mind the images that I had just witnessed. After hours of such anguish, I was utterly drained and thankfully fell asleep.

When I woke, I saw that the candle in my room was lit and my dinner was on the bedside table. I tried the door, intending to go back to the library. It was locked. I felt too poorly to do anything other than nibble at the food and lie down once more.

During that night, I had little rest. A persistent scraping noise seemed to surround me, accompanied by a foul odor that irritated my nose and throat. Yet I could find no cause of the sound or the stench.

In the morning, my breakfast was on the hall table as usual. I left it untouched and went straight to the library. I was determined to prove to myself that *The Pope Maze* was just an unpleasant publication that I had no cause to fear. It may well have revolted and unbalanced me like no other book before; but I needed to be rational and find it again to obtain some degree of comprehension about what it meant. I felt obliged to do so as a professional bibliophile.

The Pope Maze was not where I had left it. I spent the next hour searching thoroughly and even removed the works I had already catalogued and placed on the shelves to see if the book was behind them. It was nowhere to be found.

I finally ate my breakfast and returned, without enthusiasm, to my usual duties. I brooded about *The Pope Maze*. Above all, I could not understand what those vile drawings and scrawled comments in the second half of the book had to do with a maze.

In the late afternoon, I decided that I needed to speak to Miss Pope. I propped open the library door with a heavy volume and positioned a chair so that I could see her when she arrived with my dinner. However, my state of nervous excitement proved to be too great and I drifted off to sleep. It was Miss Pope's voice that roused me.

"I assume that you're waiting for me?"

I rose and went into the hall.

"Yes. I found a book. About a maze. It was bizarre ..."

THE MAZE

I paused. Miss Pope had narrowed her eyes, accentuating her stern gaze.

"You discovered the book, I know. You were never meant to. I thought my father had destroyed it long ago."

"Have you seen it?" I asked eagerly. "Those awful drawings and the meaningless words …"

Miss Pope placed the dinner tray on the hall table.

"You're upset. Eat and rest."

I was determined that she would not divert me so easily.

"The hedge outside is part of the maze, isn't it? The leaves are blood red. I can't find any reference to such hedging in your books on horticulture. So where did the hedge come from?"

"Forget the book," Miss Pope said and looked straight at me. "You should leave first thing tomorrow morning. There's a train just after nine o'clock. Thank you for your work. Send me your bill when you reach home."

"I haven't finished the task you set."

"No matter," Miss Pope replied firmly.

She picked up the dinner tray and shepherded me into my room. Having placed down the tray, she left hurriedly, closing the door behind her and leaving it unlocked.

I listened to the footsteps receding down the hall and resolved to explore the house to search for *The Pope Maze*. I knew that doing so would anger Miss Pope; on the other hand, I reasoned that she had already dismissed me.

I moved quietly into the hall. There were no stairs near here but my intention was to find some.

I conjectured that if Miss Pope had hidden the book, assuming that she had retained it, she would likely have put it in an attic or basement.

The corridors off the hall were still lit by candles. I set off, treading as softly as I could. The hopelessness of my task soon became apparent, though. There were no stairs to be seen. I also found that no matter which way I turned and which corridor I took, I ended back in the hall. Moreover, and this was particularly disturbing, I could see no doors along the corridors.

The second time that I found myself in the hall again, I decided to pause in my search and eat. I was not worried that my dinner was cold; I was too busy trying to work out where I had gone wrong in my wanderings about the building. With a shock, I also became aware that I was talking to myself.

This is ridiculous, I decided. I need to settle down and proceed logically.

Once I had finished my meal, I strode to the corridor by the side of the library door. I continued down it until the end and noticed, for the first time, one of the building's small windows. I tried to peer out into the late summer's evening. All I could see was the blood-red mass of the hedge: Clearly, I was by an outside wall. I made a mental note of my location and walked down a corridor that appeared to run along the outer wall. At the end, I paused, made a further mental note of my progress, and took a corridor that seemed to lead into the middle of the house.

I had gone no more than a few steps when I passed a door. I thought that I had come this way earlier and wondered how I could have missed such an obvious feature. I was sure there had been no doors in the corridors before now. I was debating whether to try the handle when a noise stole my attention.

I moved closer to one of the door's panels and listened. Two men were speaking in low tones on the other side.

"No," one said. "A garrote is best. I know someone who will gladly perform the task. The crowd will love the spectacle."

"I'm not so sure," the other replied. "Hanging is always popular. What's more, people expect to see a hanging."

I frowned, unable to rationalize what I had heard. These two must be joking, I surmised. Or perhaps they're reading the lines from a play. Either way, what is absolutely certain is that I am not alone in the house with Miss Pope.

When I knocked lightly, the voices went silent, so I knocked harder. There was no reply. I grasped the handle and pushed it down.

The door sprang open, releasing a gust of putrid air. I bent forward and coughed to rid my mouth of the foul taste. As I did so, the air changed direction and pulled at me. I stumbled into the room and collapsed, the door closing behind me with a crash.

The room was in complete darkness, and I listened for the voices that I had heard earlier. There was only silence. Yet this was not the quietude of any room that I had ever been in; the stillness had a depth that stretched into the gloom, suggesting that I was in the midst of a void without bounds.

My hands stuck to the floor so I could not rise. Each time I moved, a sulfurous smell rose and made the skin on my face prickle with sweat.

"Hello," I called out in desperation.

My voice echoed back, growing quieter with each reiteration. No one responded.

I turned my head this way and that, craning for a chink of light. After a while, the blackness in front began to lighten. A path appeared between two tall blood-red hedges. Above them, the evening sky was a delicate shade of pink.

I'm in the maze, I discerned with sudden clarity. I'm in the maze at sunset.

Glancing behind, I saw that a hedge had replaced the door, blocking me in. Whatever substance had been on the ground beneath me was gone. My hands were resting, palms downward, on beaten earth. I cautiously inhaled. The air was fresh and pleasantly warm.

I rose and walked slowly between the hedges, for I had nowhere else to go.

As I progressed, I heard a cry and quickened my pace. Next came what sounded like a series of heavy objects falling. This was followed by dust billowing from a gap in the hedge.

I ran to the gap. Through the dust I could see that I was at the end of a narrow street. On either side, the buildings were fragmenting, their timber and masonry disintegrating. And there, among the falling debris, was a child, a girl, crying for help.

The girl was about thirty yards away. I shouted and gestured for her to come to me. She continued crying and did not move. The buildings between us were rupturing.

The girl cried out again.

"I'm coming," I shouted and sprinted into the mayhem.

When the girl saw what I was doing, she turned away.

'Wait!" I yelled. "Stay there."

The girl walked straight into the trajectory of a falling beam. I leaped to save her and tripped on a chunk of broken stonework. I heard a terrible cacophony above me, twisted onto my back, and watched helplessly as a shower of bricks and plaster plummeted onto my left leg. The pain was so great, I passed out.

I have no idea how much time went by. When I regained consciousness, I moved with care, expecting to be buried beneath the shattered buildings. But I was no longer among them. I stood up awkwardly, my leg throbbing. I was back between the hedges. I gazed at my clothes. There was no sign of dust, no tears in the fabric.

What had just happened? I asked myself. *And what had become of that poor girl?*

My recent experience made no sense. I knew that I had another priority, however: I needed to escape from the maze. Then, unquestionably, I had to leave Miss Pope and her monstrous home.

I found myself at a crossroads. Each of the four paths looked identical. I glanced at the sky; unfortunately, it held no clue to my position. The stars were not out; there was simply the red hue of the disappearing sun.

My choice of direction was made for me, though. When I looked again at the paths, three of them were no longer empty. On each was an identical figure, wearing a bloodstained butcher's apron and carrying one of the tools of the slaughterer's trade: a cleaver. Together, the three gruesome forms stared at me, their faces distorted by unnaturally wide grins.

An awful sensation of ice-cold biliousness passed through me. Struggling against the pain in my leg, I turned to the remaining path and began to limp down it. Behind me, the butchers called out to one another and gave chase.

I had covered no more than fifty yards when I glanced up and found a hedge unexpectedly barring my way. There was no sign of an exit. I turned. The three butchers were there, one behind the other. They looked delighted, knowing that I was trapped.

Nothing in my life had prepared me to face such an assault. The first butcher came close—I could smell rancid meat on his breath—and brought his cleaver down across my face. I cried out and raised my hand to the blood welling from my cheek.

The second butcher jostled the first out of the way. I felt immeasurable anxiety as I watched him raise his cleaver. With a laugh echoed by his companions, he slashed my other cheek. I fell back against the hedge and sank to the ground.

Now the third butcher wanted his turn. He elbowed the other two back and stood above me, examining my neck and shoulders, his cleaver hanging loose at his side. At that instant, I was

THE MAZE

filled with a desperate desire to survive. I kicked out at the butcher with my good leg. The sole of my shoe caught the hand clutching the cleaver and sent the deadly implement spinning away. For a second, all three butchers looked confused. I seized my chance, grabbed at the hedge and hauled myself up. Gritting my teeth, I threw myself against the nearest butcher, succeeded in knocking him against the others, and hobbled back the way I had come. My assailants shouted fiercely but I ignored them. Blood from the wounds on my face trickled into my mouth and caused me to cough and spit. However, I did not stop.

The crossroads had gone and the hedges appeared to hem me in. Strangely, when I reached the end of this blind alley, a new path immediately opened up to the side. I took it without hesitating.

Each path I limped down seemed blocked in a similar way. A further path then providentially materialized at the last moment, taking me in another direction. Each of these paths was becoming shorter in length and it occurred to me that perhaps I was nearing the center of the maze rather than the exit. But the maze gave me no choice of direction. And all this time, the butchers persisted in their pursuit, shouting unintelligibly to each other.

The sky was now darkening. I slowed, gasping for breath. My life, it would seem, was hurtling toward an ignoble finale.

Just as I lost all hope, I saw a glow emanating ahead of me. I had no idea what it meant. I shrugged, moved feebly towards it and halted.

I had entered a cobbled square. Lights bulbs were strung between trees, casting a yellow radiance. On each of the square's sides were brick-built homes and businesses, while in the middle a fountain stood, water flowing from gargoyles' mouths. One of the businesses, a café, was open. A waiter in a black apron beckoned to me.

I glanced behind. A butcher's premises stood where the path had been. A sign in the window stated that the shop was closed. I looked carefully around. Other than the waiter, there was no sign of anyone.

My fatigue was extreme. I accepted the waiter's invitation and walked unevenly to the café. I lowered myself into a wicker chair, keeping my wounded leg stretched, and closed my eyes while I brought my labored breathing back under control. Once I felt calmer, I took a handful of paper napkins from the table by my side and dabbed cautiously at the stinging wounds on my face. The blood had stopped oozing and was beginning to coagulate.

With a gentle rattle of porcelain, the waiter placed a cup and saucer on the table. I could smell the strong aroma of coffee.

I nodded my thanks. The waiter moved away and looked impassively across the square. I sipped the coffee. Despite my preference for tea, it tasted good. I felt myself relaxing and followed the waiter's gaze. He was staring at a clock set into a church tower. As I took another sip of my drink, the clock began to strike twelve.

Is it really midnight?

THE MAZE

A desperate need for sleep was overpowering me. I shook my head and took a last gulp of the coffee as the clock finished its twelfth strike. At that precise moment, the double doors at the front of the church opened.

In an attempt to stay awake, I concentrated on the procession that started to appear. It consisted of six pallbearers, carrying a casket at shoulder height, followed by a single line of solemn-looking men and women clothed in black. No one made a sound.

I tried to turn my head to the waiter to ask what was happening and found that I was unable to move my neck. In panic, I endeavored to stand. My body would not respond. My arms and legs were fixed in position, the muscles rigid. With effort, I looked down at the dregs of the coffee and knew, instinctively, that the waiter had drugged me.

I managed to force my eyes up again. Powerless, I watched the cortège approach the café. The pallbearers lowered the casket, while the others waited patiently. At the same time, the drug was mastering my mind. I was sinking into a mental abyss and could barely see the pallbearers as they opened the casket. It was empty. Their purpose was clear: They intended to bury me. I screamed but I doubt that I made any noise. I was almost completely subdued. My last sense to retain any capability was my hearing. As oblivion overwhelmed me, I heard a shout, followed by what could have been the crack of a whip.

I came to in the library. Whether hours or days later, I do not know. I was lying sideways on a couch, facing the door. The woodwork and brass handle were blurred and distorted. I closed my eyes tight and reopened them. The door was in focus and no longer warped. I tried to move and felt an ache in my leg. I lay back and ran one hand slowly across my face. Cloth pads were taped across both cheeks.

After a long while, I pushed myself upright and heard a clattering sound. I moaned in disbelief as I saw that a metal bracelet encircled each of my wrists. From a ring on each bracelet, a chain curved up towards the ceiling. Here, the two ends were attached to rails that ran the length of the room.

Over the next hour or so, I discovered that the chains gave me sufficient freedom to hobble to any part of the room. My first goal was to try the door. It was fastened, as I had suspected. On a table by the door stood a carafe of water, a bowl of fruit and a plate of cheese and bread. In a far corner was a washstand with a jug of water and a towel. The presence of the water made me aware of the sweat and grime that clung uncomfortably to me. I peeled away the cloth dressings on my face and washed, the chains clinking with my every movement. Afterwards, behind a curtain, I found a bucket, presumably left there for the receipt of my bodily waste.

Everything I require is here, I realized grimly, including a lifetime of reading material.

On the desk was a note.

I trust you agree that you are fortunate. I succeeded in removing you from the maze before you were buried, comatose and helpless. I have checked your wounds. I believe they will heal. The scars will remain and your leg may continue to trouble you a little.

My family has preserved the secret of the maze for over two hundred years. Regrettably, you have interfered. You now understand how the Pope Maze can entangle you in violent horror, as the book suggested. Of course, you failed to appreciate this at the time.

You cannot return with such a secret to the world you once knew. Some people would regard you as mad; others would investigate and, armed with their naïve incomprehension, invade my home. I cannot allow this.

I have arranged for your death notice to be placed in the newspapers. My enquiries indicate that you have no immediate relatives, so I do not expect any unwanted investigation. Thus, as far as anyone else is concerned, you are no more. Please feel free to continue your work in the library. Once you have finished, I suggest that you read. You enjoy reading, do you not?

Miss Pope

I screwed up the note, threw it across the room and pulled open the desk's drawers. Whether or not Miss Pope deliberately left me the paper and pencils that I found, I may never know. Whatever her motivation, I have used them to write this account. I suspect that no one will ever read about my ordeal. Or if you have, you may not believe it. But I beg you to accept what I have written as the truth. You must then do the world an immense service. You must destroy the house and the maze. Destroy them as soon as you can.

ABOUT THE AUTHORS

Gregg Chamberlain ives in rural Canada with missus, Anne, and a clowder of cats. Multiple short-fiction credits in the speculative fiction genres.

Originally from Los Angeles, Pedro Iniguez now lives in Sioux Falls, South Dakota. He spends his time reading, writing, and painting, which stems from his childhood love of science-fiction, horror, and comic books.

He has appeared alongside such authors as Dennis Etchison, Ramsey Campbell, Joe R. Lansdale, Lisa Morton, Nick Mamatas, Brian Evenson, Ken Liu, Kate Wilhelm, and Tim Pratt.

His work can be found in magazines and anthologies such as *Space and Time Magazine*, *Crossed Genres*, *Dig Two Graves*, *Writers of Mystery and Imagination*, *Deserts of Fire*, and *Altered States II*.

His cyberpunk novel, *Control Theory*, was released in 2016 and his 10-year collection, *Synthetic Dawns & Crimson Dusks*, was released in 2020.

Gordon Grice has written about the dark corners of biology for *The New Yorker* (where he tackled the history of post-mortem dissections), *Harper's* (black widow spiders), and *Discover* (leprosy). He also writes horror stories, including the Best of the 'Net winner "The White Cat" and the Year's Best Fantasy and Horror runner-up "Hide."

The Frightening Floyds are authors and small press owners from Louisville, KY where they live with their two dogs (Tarzan and Pegasus) and four cats (Baloo, Narnia, Pandy, and Baby Bat). They don't own any sloths – mutant-zombie or regular.

Kenneth Bykerk lives in the ghost town of Howells, Arizona, the suburb of the ghost town of Walker, AZ on the creek where the gold was found that brought recognition of Territorial status to the land. His days spent free from the real world often find him hiking through the ruins and forgotten graveyards that surround his mountain home. Experiencing the first of hopefully many 2nd childhoods, he has taken to writing down the musings inspired by his hikes to lost mines or his midnight strolls through the remains of Howells. "Child of the Earth" is one of 33 stories he has produced these last four years. These 33 stories are collectively known as *The Tales of the Bajazid*.

Other than "Child of the Earth", four others have been sold with one, "Kachina", appearing in the February 2018 issue of *WeirdBook* #38 and, "Mercy Holds No Measure" in the upcoming *WeirdBook 2018* annual. "Where Lies Hope" appears in the November 2018 issue of *WeirdMask* and "The Woman in the Tree" in Tell-Tale Press 2018 Winter Holidays edition, *The Blood Tomes*.

The Tales of the Bajazid chronicles the history of one of the many ghost towns in the mountains of central Arizona. One day while showing a friend the ruins of the smelter walking distance down the creek, he was asked why so much concrete was used to seal the entrance. The ruins he had played upon as a child, that his grandmother had played upon as a child, transformed before his eyes as each collapsed and hidden adit or old shaft hopefully filled began telling stories only he could hear. Following the advice of write what you know, with his changed perspective, those places he played as a child still serve to inspire hours of time lost to forest trails but now in ways that child of yore would probably be disturbed by. That kid was a scaredy-cat.

Angela Yuriko Smith is an American poet, publisher, and author. Her first collection of poetry, In Favor of Pain, was nominated for a 2017 Elgin Award. Her novella, Bitter Suites, is a 2018 Bram Stoker Awards® Finalist. In 2019 she won the SFPA's poetry contest in the dwarf form category. She has been nominated for a 2020 Pushcart Prize.

Stanley is a resident of New York State. He and his family live in an antique farm house near Lake Ontario. Stanley wasted much of his youth watching monster movies, reading science fiction, drawing pictures and writing stories. Many of his tales have appeared in magazines and anthologies, including Gypsum Sound Tales' "COLP: A Little Bit of Nonsense", "Haunted life" from Alban Lake Publishing, and "Starship Logs" from Tell-Tale Press. His bibliography may be viewed on his website at: stanleybwebbauthor.wordpress.com, or his Author Central page at: amazon.com/author/stanleywebb.

Stanley thanks everyone who has ever read his work.

Pamela K. Kinney is an award winning published author of horror, science fiction, fantasy, poetry, and a ghost wrangler of nonfiction ghost books published by Schiffer Publishing. Her horror short story, "Bottled Spirits" published by *Buzzymag.com* was runner up for the 2013 Small Press Award.

William D Carl lives in Pawtucket, R.I., and is a horror/thriller novelist. His first book, BESTIAL (Book one in the Werepocalypse Saga) is now available from Crossroad Press. Book 2, PRIMEVAL, has also been released. Look for his Euro-horror homage THE SCHOOL THAT SCREAMED from Necon e-book contemporary horror as well as his terrifying OUT OF THE WOODS from Post Mortem Press. His new series, GONE NOIR, has just commenced with the first book, THREE DAYS GONE, which follows the adventures of a private detective who gets all the weirdest cases in Cincinnati, Ohio. He has published short fiction in over twenty five anthologies and magazines, and he writes a column called Bill's Bizarre Bijou for *Cinema Knife Fight* in which he talks about the strangest movies you've never seen. He lives with his partner of 26 years and one rather large hound dog. He likes pie.

Matthew M. Montelione is a horror writer and historian born and raised in New York. His work has been published in many titles, including *Quoth the Raven: A Contemporary Reimagining of the Works of Edgar Allan Poe* and *LOVE: A Dark Microfiction Anthology*.

R.C. Mulhare has the distinction of reading a translation of the famous cursed play "The King in Yellow" without going mad, once successfully defended her day-job workplace from zombies, through some judicious use of clearance-rack garden tools, and fought off a group of Yog-Sothoth cultists in the hallway of a hotel in Providence, Rhode Island.

K.J Watson's fiction and non-fiction have appeared on the radio, in magazines and comics, and on websites. He has won a Sweek Best Story Award and *Communicator* magazine's Article of the Year Award.

ALSO AVAILABLE FROM NIGHTMARE PRESS:

Whoops! I Woke the Dead by Joseph Rubas: A girl with a spellbook accidentally wakes the dead on Halloween night.

THE VAMPIRE SERIES OF EXTREME HORROR
by Todd Sullivan

Butchers: Vampires hunting vampires in this no-holds-barred bloodfest set in Korea.

The Gray Man of Smoke and Shadows: A rogue vampire seeks revenge on her abusive uncle while another vampire hunts her.

OTHER BOOKS

Night of the Possums by Jacob Floyd: Man becomes roadkill as mutant possums rise up and attack the populace of a small Kentucky town.

Chainsaw Sisters by Jacob Floyd: An amnesiac woman believes her dead sister is talking to her through a chainsaw, asking her to seek revenge against the men who murdered her.

COMING SOON FROM NIGHTMARE PRESS:

The Cursed Diary of a Brooklyn Dog Walker
Michael Reyes

The Untaken
Bekki Pate

All Roads Lead
Jennifer Winters

Viva La Muerte
Quinn Hernandez

In Dormancy, They Sleep
D.G. Sutter

Todd Sullivan Presents: The Vampire Connoisseur
A vampire anthology

Slaughter at Seabridge
Cassidy Frost

The Passing
Joseph Rubas

Horrifica
Sheldon Woodbury

Made in the USA
Middletown, DE
13 September 2021